Two Gentlemen of Corona

by Jim Geoghan

A SAMUEL FRENCH ACTING EDITION

SAMUEL FRENCH

FOUNDED 1830

NEW YORK HOLLYWOOD LONDON TORONTO

SAMUELFRENCH.COM

ISBN 978-0-573-69866-8   Printed in U.S.A.   #29265

MUSIC USE NOTE

IMPORTANT BILLING AND CREDIT
REQUIREMENTS

TWO GENTLEMEN OF CORONA was first produced by Dana Reynolds and Richard Israel, West Coast Ensemble, at the Lyric-Hyperion theatre in Los Angeles on June 24, 2005. The performance was directed by Henry Polic II, with sets by Tim Farmer, costumes by Shon LeBlanc, lighting by Lisa D. Katz, sound by Bryce Ryness, and choreography by Cate Caplin. The Production Stage Manager was J.T. Dewart. The cast was as follows:

JOEY BROCCO	Adrian R'Mante
PHIL	Phillip C. Curry
CARMINE FABIANO	Chris Damiano
JOHN ESPOSITO	Sam Ingraffia
ANGELINA FRATIANO	C.B. Spencer
LENNY GREEN	Michael Zemenick

CHARACTERS

JOEY BROCCO – Low-level member of a New York crime family. Twenties, handsome, clever, resourceful, street wise, heart of a poet, a romantic, excellent dancer.

CARMINE FABIANO – Equally low-level member of a New York crime family. Twenties, lifelong friend of Joey's, not nearly as smart or good-looking but good hearted.

JOHN ESPOSITO – High ranking under boss of a New York crime family. Late forties, fifties, dresses well, wealthy, powerful, elegant, pompous.

ANGELINA FRATIANO – Twenties, John Esposito's mistress, working class, beautiful, smart and getting smarter. Excellent dancer.

PHIL WILLIAMS – African-American, forties or fifties. Hard working, blue collar, quiet and level headed.

LENNY GREEN – Forties or fifties, overweight, fussy, mild mannered, sweet natured.

For Genevieve,

who started doing plays for me when she was four.

ACT ONE

(The set is a classic chrome diner from the early nineteen sixties somewhere in Corona, Queens.)

(The diner is a perfect time capsule of working class New York forty years ago. It has a counter with stools, tables and chairs [or booths], a period juke box, cigarette machine, gumball machine, cash register, doors that lead to bathrooms, a phone booth, placards that offer a steak dinner for two dollars, ads for Balantine Beer and Pall Mall Cigarettes, a poster of "Miss Reingold" for 1963 and a door that leads to the parking lot.)

(The neon sign tells us this diner is "CLOSED." It will always be closed.)

(It's also Christmas Eve and period Christmas decorations accent the diner.)

(It's two a.m. **JOEY BROCCO** *(aka* **JOEY NICKELS***) in his twenties, and a small time soldier in one of New York's organized crime families, has been loading new records into the open juke box. A popular song from 1963 [something like, "Calendar Girl," "Be My Baby," "Baby Workout," etc.] begins to play.)**

(JOEY *can't help but dance to the song. He dances quite well. He is remarkable, in fact, for someone who is not a dancer by profession.)*

(Meanwhile **PHIL**, *an African-American in his fifties, the diner's night cook, leans on the counter reading that day's* Daily News. *He watches* **JOEY** *dance for several beats and smiles.)*

PHIL. Yeah.

JOEY. You like?

---

*Please see Music Use Note on page 3.

PHIL. Very nice.

JOEY. Watch this.

> (**JOEY** *does a particularly nice move.*)
>
> Huh?

PHIL. You dance like a colored man.

JOEY. That's high praise, Phil. High praise.

> (**PHIL** *steps out from behind the counter.*)

PHIL. Step aside, youngblood. Lemme show you a few things.

> (**PHIL** *shows* **JOEY** *a dance step or two, more soul than rock 'n roll.* **JOEY** *likes what he sees and copies it. They dance like this for several beats.*)

Huh? See? First you make the move…then you keep it smooth…

JOEY. Love that. I got it…I got…

PHIL. Now these are secret Negro steps. Don't tell no one where you got 'em.

JOEY. No one finds out, Phil. How am I doin'? Any pointers?

PHIL. Just one. When you dance…

JOEY. Yeah?

PHIL. Try and find the black man inside you.

JOEY. How the hell do I do that?

PHIL. Pretend you make love to noisy women and live in a bad neighborhood.

> (*They both laugh.*)

JOEY. I'll do that. Just like you said.

> (**PHIL** *goes back behind the counter as* **JOEY** *continues to dance.* **CARMINE FABIANO** *[aka* **CARMINE THE CAMEL**] *enters. He watches* **JOEY** *dance for a beat or two.*)

CARMINE. What are you doin'?

JOEY. What's it look like?

CARMINE. Stop that!

JOEY. I can't help it. I'm happy.

CARMINE. This is Queens! Nobody's happy!

JOEY. Aw, c'mon!

CARMINE. What if John saw you dance like that?

JOEY. John's gonna get mad just because I'm dancin'?

CARMINE. No, not because you're dancin'. Because you're dancin' alone! People don't dance *alone*! They do it *with* someone! C'mon, stop that before people start talkin'! They'll think you're turnin' homo or somethin'.

(**JOEY** *stops dancing. Somewhere during the following the music will fade out.*)

JOEY. Don't you ever do that? You hear a song so good you just gotta dance to it? Even if you're alone?

CARMINE. Two things I don't do alone. I don't dance alone, I don't fuck alone.

JOEY. That's not what I hear. I hear you been goin' steady with your right hand since high school.

CARMINE. You gavone!

(*They playfully box with each other.*)

JOEY. I hope you were gentle when you broke the news to your *left* hand!

CARMINE. I'll show ya my left hand.

JOEY. "Sorry, left hand but my right hand does a better job. Let's just be friends from now on, okay?"

CARMINE. Fuckin' guy!

JOEY. Douchebag!

CARMINE. Asshole!

JOEY. Jerk off!

CARMINE. You're demented, you know that! Demented!

JOEY. I oughta...

CARMINE. You oughta what! I got moves, baby!

JOEY. The only move you got left is shufflin' off to the toilet!

(**CARMINE** *breaks out laughing.*)

CARMINE. Hah! That's funny! The toilet! Love this guy!

(*beat*)

Hey, Phil you hear what Joey said?

PHIL. (*not looking up*) I didn't hear nothin'.

CARMINE. (*re:* **PHIL**) I love this guy! If I'm ever on trial I want him on the witness stand!

JOEY. How was your trip? How was South Carolina?

CARMINE. Aw, please! Wall to wall hicks an' hillbillies! You should come with me someday. See for yourself. Everyone down there marries their own sister and has kids.

JOEY. It can't be that bad.

CARMINE. Picture an entire state where everyone owns one pair of pants and has a bad haircut. And those are the *women.*

JOEY. C'mon!

CARMINE. And the food they eat! Okra, you ever hear of okra?

JOEY. No.

CARMINE. I think it's a vegetable.

PHIL. It's a fish.

CARMINE. Okra's a fish?

PHIL. Nasty ass, bad smellin' fish.

CARMINE. No wonder I hate it so much. But they eat okra by the ton. And greasy meat that's still on the bone. You could *die* before you find a restaurant that serves veal Parmesan or lasagna! And the music they listen to. Holy shit! I got a dog, I got a truck, you left him for me so I'm leavin' her for you!

PHIL. (*joking*) I love that song.

CARMINE. Half these people can't even read or write their own name but it works out seein' as how most of them are named "Goober." And stupid? Jesus! One of them told me he thought daylight savings was a *bank*! Christ, these hillbillies are dumber than a block of provolone. But not your family, Phil. I'm talkin' about white people here.

PHIL. I figured that out. My family's been called a lot of things but "hillbilly" ain't one of them.

CARMINE. Before I forget… Phil, your family says hello and wishes you a merry Christmas.

PHIL. Thanks. You give 'em the presents and the money?

CARMINE. Yeah. And your sister's lookin' better an' better every time I see her.

PHIL. Careful, youngblood. Once you go black…

CARMINE. I know. I mean, I've heard. And she can cook, too. Better than you at least. She makes this thing with biscuits and gravy. What's that called?

PHIL. Biscuits and gravy.

CARMINE. Figures.

(CARMINE hands PHIL a wrapped present.)

Here, almost forgot. Your sister said she knitted this for you. Feels like gloves.

PHIL. Scarf. It's always a scarf.

(PHIL puts the present away.)

Thanks for doing that, Carmine. You hungry? Want something to eat?

CARMINE. Naw. I had pizza in Baltimore. Tell you what, a cup of coffee.

PHIL. Coffee.

CARMINE. And give it a little bah-boom.

JOEY. Make mine a bah-boom, hold the coffee.

(PHIL pours and serves the drinks in coffee cups, then returns to his newspaper during the following.)

CARMINE. Listen, Joey I hope you don't mind I dropped by your house, unloaded forty cases of Tennessee whiskey.

JOEY. Did my mother see?

CARMINE. Of course she did. She had to open the garage for me.

JOEY. Aw, Jesus. What'd she say?

CARMINE. She said she wanted a case of whiskey for herself. I tried to get her to take less but she wouldn't budge.

JOEY. She's sweet but ruthless.

CARMINE. I told her I thought she was bein' a little greedy and she hit me in the nuts with her cane so hard, I swear I'll never have children.

JOEY. If it was so much trouble why didn't you just leave them on the truck?

CARMINE. Are you kiddin'? What if John swung by and saw I was runnin' hootch on the side!

JOEY. So instead it's in my garage now?

CARMINE. It'll be there a day, maybe two.

JOEY. Man, you gotta be careful with that, Carmine. If John ever found out.

CARMINE. John's not going to find out.

JOEY. But if he did…

CARMINE. He won't! I was in and out of your garage in five minutes! Nobody saw nothin'.

JOEY. Dominick help you?

CARMINE. Hmm?

JOEY. Dominick, did he help you unload the cases of whiskey?

CARMINE. *(uncomfortable)* Dominick, uh… No.

JOEY. He went with you, didn't he?

CARMINE. Dominick?

JOEY. No, the Queen of frikkin' England! Yes, Dominick. He went along on this trip, didn't he?

CARMINE. Yeah, Dom came along. Part of the trip.

JOEY. What do you mean "part of the trip?"

CARMINE. Well, Dominick went down to South Carolina… but…

JOEY. But what.

CARMINE. Let's just say Dominick is still in South Carolina.

JOEY. How much longer is he gonna be there?

(No reply.)

How much longer?

(No reply.)

A few days?

(No reply.)

Longer?

CARMINE. Yeah. Longer.

*(**JOEY** finally understands.)*

JOEY. No…

(beat)

Really?

*(**CARMINE** nods.)*

Goddamn! Not Dominick! No! Not Dominick! We grew up together! We were in first grade together! I've known him my whole life! No, no, not Dominick! No! Not him! Not Dominick!

CARMINE. Had to be done.

JOEY. Dominick! No!

CARMINE. Nothin' I could do.

JOEY. But… Aw for Christ sake!

CARMINE. It's done, Joey.

JOEY. Dominick?!

CARMINE. It's done.

JOEY. His mother! Oh, God! What about his mother!

CARMINE. I didn't have to kill her. Only Dominick.

JOEY. She'll be heart broken. Totally shocked.

CARMINE. Shocked? Her son sleeps with two handguns and uses her Tupperware to mix heroin at her kitchen table and she's gonna be shocked?

JOEY. Is that what it was? The drug stuff?

CARMINE. I told him to stop. You told him to stop. I'll bet you Phil told him to stop, too.

PHIL. I didn't tell him nothin'.

CARMINE. Still, we all know the rule. Dominick knew the rule, too. C'mon. No way John was gonna turn a blind eye to that.

JOEY. Then the order came from John?

CARMINE. Even higher. Vincent.

JOEY. Vincent? Jeez! The capo di tutti capi?

CARMINE. Boss of bosses. John had a sit down with Vincent at Vincent's favorite steak house. Very elegant setting. Very formal. Table cloth, cloth napkins…If you're drinkin' red wine and switch to white they put it in another glass. This was very high level stuff. Wasn't nothin' I could do.

JOEY. So you went down to South Carolina with Dominick knowing…

CARMINE. Yeah. And it wasn't an easy trip, lemme tell yuh. Having Dominick in the truck with you is like drivin' with a ten year-old. "Are we there yet? Are we there yet?" And we're still in New Jersey! I hate that. Takin' a long drive with someone knowin' you're comin' back alone. It almost ruined my whole trip.

JOEY. Where'd you do it? Out in the middle of nowhere?

CARMINE. Pretty much. The great thing about South Carolina is you're never more than five minutes away from the middle of nowhere. "C'mon, Dominick. There's these three sisters. They live in a cabin, way in the woods. They're eighteen and gorgeous. Long legs, tits out to here. And they're nymphos. Yeah, they *like* it! They can't get enough of it! C'mon, just a little bit more. They live right down here in a cabin. C'mon, this way." Dom looks in the woods, then he goes, he goes, "Wait! I think I can see 'em! Yeah, I think I can see 'em! Holy shit, I see the nymphos!" Bang!

JOEY. Then he died happy.

CARMINE. Big smile on his face.

JOEY. That was nice of you.

CARMINE. It was the least I could do.

(**PHIL** *crosses to* **CARMINE** *and* **JOEY** *to refill their cups with more whiskey.*)

PHIL. Dominick?

JOEY. Yeah...

CARMINE. Had to be done, Phil. Wasn't nothin' I could do.

JOEY. You feel bad, Phil?

PHIL. Of course. The part of me that liked Dominick feels *real* bad. But...

JOEY. But what?

PHIL. The part of me that owed Dominick a hundred dollars don't feel bad at all. It's the money you gave my sister. Damn!

JOEY. What?

PHIL. I should've borrowed more.

JOEY. The family's not gonna get anywhere if we keep this up. You make one mistake, then you pay for it with your life.

CARMINE. *(shrugs)* It's our tradition.

JOEY. Well, it's a bad one.

PHIL. The Yakuza.

CARMINE. The whoza?

PHIL. The Yakuza. When I was a supply sergeant stationed in Japan you couldn't move anything that was black market without dealing with the Yakuza. They're what you guys are.

CARMINE. You mean wise guys?

PHIL. Exactly. But they're Japanese.

CARMINE. Holy shit.

JOEY. Japanese wiseguys?

PHIL. And they go way back, too. Centuries. Secret ceremonies, tattoos, the works. But if someone screws up in the Yakuza, they don't get a bullet in the head. They've got this whole "I'm sorry I screwed up" ceremony.

JOEY. No way.

CARMINE. You're kiddin'.

PHIL. They go to their boss and *beg* for his mercy. They go "I'm sorry I screwed up. I really screwed up. I promise I won't screw up no more." Then they take out a knife and, as a gesture of how serious they are about this thing...

JOEY. Yeah?

PHIL. They chop off a finger.

CARMINE. Holy shit!

JOEY. Oh my God!

PHIL. Or just part of a finger. It depends on how much they fucked up. You know, a little fuck up – just the tip. A big fuck up – the whole thing. Then they all drink some sake and go bang some geisha girls. Everyone's happy, the boss is happy, the guy is happy.

CARMINE. He's happy with nine fingers.

PHIL. Some of the older guys are down to being happy with four or five fingers. It comes from years and years of saying "I'm sorry."

CARMINE. Man, the Japanese are so fucked up.

PHIL. Think about it. A man's got ten fingers but only one life.

(**PHIL** *crosses back behind the counter and resumes reading his newspaper.*)

JOEY. At least they don't wind up dead in the middle of nowhere.

(beat)

It's funny. When your time comes in this family, it usually comes from your best friend.

CARMINE. Dominick wasn't my best friend.

JOEY. I hate to tell you, Carmine...You were *his*.

CARMINE. Aw, shit. What'd you tell me that for? Now you make me feel bad. I feel very bad now.

JOEY. The person you love and trust the most is the person who leaves you dead in the woods.

CARMINE. It's our way.

JOEY. When it's time for me to go, Carmine...

CARMINE. Yeah?

JOEY. I hope it comes from you.

*(**CARMINE** is both stunned and touched.)*

CARMINE. Jesus, what a thing to say.

JOEY. It's how I feel. I'd like to see your face last. Not some stranger.

CARMINE. In that case, when it's time for me to go, I hope it comes from you.

JOEY. Really?

CARMINE. Yeah.

(They look at each other then smile tenderly.)

PHIL. That's beautiful. Just beautiful. Two best friends promising to kill each other on Christmas Eve. That oughta be a Christmas card. "Merry Christmas, I'll kill you if you kill me. And, if you live another week, Happy New Year." Just beautiful.

CARMINE. Phil's right. C'mon, this is not a time for this! It's fuckin' Christmas. It's time for hope and joy and religion. Shit like that.

*(**CARMINE** puts a nickel in the juke box, presses a button and a rock Christmas song begins to play.)*

Good things happen at Christmas! Yeah! We need to cheer this place up. C'mon. It's like a funeral in here. Love this song!

*(**CARMINE** begins to dance to the song. He's a terrible dancer.)*

Love it! And it's great to dance to.

JOEY. You dance like a printing press.

PHIL. When you went to South Carolina...

CARMINE. Yeah?

PHIL. Did a possum crawl in your pants?

CARMINE. Very funny. You watch, I'll get better.

*(**PHIL** watches **CARMINE** dance for a few beats, then.)*

PHIL. If you plan on getting better…

CARMINE. Yeah?

PHIL. You gonna use that body?

CARMINE. Huh?

PHIL. Step aside. Let me show you a few things. Damn, watchin' white people dance is painful. Hurts like a son of a bitch.

*(**PHIL** steps out behind the counter and shows **CARMINE** some dance moves.)*

See what I'm doing? This is how it goes.

CARMINE. Nice.

PHIL. See my face while I'm dancing?

CARMINE. What about it?

PHIL. See any look of pain or fear?

CARMINE. No.

PHIL. Try doin' the same thing.

*(**PHIL** continues to show **CARMINE** some dance steps. **JOEY** joins in, then **CARMINE**. **PHIL** and **JOEY** are doing a great job. **CARMINE**'s dancing is still terrible. The three men continue to dance in unison for several beats when…)*

*(**JOEY** and **PHIL** see **JOHN ESPOSITO** about to enter. They exchange looks of warning and stop dancing. They don't warn **CARMINE**, however, and **CARMINE** continues to dance.)*

CARMINE. Uh huh…yeah…I got it now…yeah, okay…

*(**JOHN ESPOSITO** enters. **JOHN** is a powerful under boss in this crime family. He doesn't bother to hold the door open for…)*

*(**ANGELINA FRATIANO**, his mistress more than thirty years his junior. **ANGELINA**, attractive despite big hair,*

too much makeup, jewelry and a fur coat, has to struggle to push the door open and enter after **JOHN.**)

JOHN. Carmine! What are you doin'?

(**CARMINE** *stops dancing. The song fades out during the following.*)

CARMINE. John. Oh, I was just dancin' is all.

JOHN. Alone? You don't dance alone. You dance *with* someone.

JOEY. That's what we've been tellin' him.

PHIL. Maybe he'll listen to you, John.

(**JOEY** *and* **PHIL** *exchange furtive smirks.*)

JOHN. Stop doin' shit like that. That's not right. People will talk. They'll say you're homo or somethin'. You're not turnin' homo on us, are you?

(**CARMINE** *grabs his crotch.*)

CARMINE. Are you kiddin'? Hey, c'mon. The crack of dawn ain't safe!

JOEY. We didn't expect to see you. Merry Christmas, John.

CARMINE. Yeah, Merry Christmas.

JOHN. Yeah. Yeah.

(**JOHN** *exchanges hugs and wiseguy kisses with* **CARMINE** *and* **JOEY.** *Meanwhile,* **ANGELINA** *stands nearby holding some envelopes.*)

Carmine, you seein' your mother tomorrow?

CARMINE. Seeing my mother? Are you serious? I'd rather have a rusty nail jammed up my eye.

(*off* **JOHN** *'s look*)

Uh…yeah, John. Of course. It's Christmas Day. I'll do that. I'll go visit my mother.

JOHN. You be sure and see her now.

CARMINE. I will.

JOHN. I'm going to call her. I'm going to ask if you were there.

CARMINE. You'll do it, too!

JOHN. You'd better believe. Angelina!

> (ANGELINA *flips through the envelopes, finds the one she's looking for, crosses to* CARMINE *and hands it to him.*)

This is for you, Carmine.

ANGELINA. John Esposito wishes you a very merry Christmas and a New Year that is both healthy and prosperous.

CARMINE. John, I don't know what to say!

JOHN. Don't say nothin'.

> (JOHN *puts his arm around* CARMINE *and takes him aside.*)

Just tell me about your trip to North Carolina.

CARMINE. South Carolina.

JOHN. What?

CARMINE. It's where I go. Twice a week. Not North Carolina, South Carolina.

JOHN. There's a difference?

CARMINE. I guess not.

JOHN. You had a good trip?

CARMINE. Yeah.

JOHN. I mean, everything worked out?

CARMINE. Oh yeah.

JOHN. The thing I asked you to take care of?

CARMINE. It was taken care of.

JOHN. Nothin' the cops could come at us with someday?

CARMINE. Naw, the gun I used is in twelve pieces in five states. And there's no blood in the truck. I did it out in the woods. Way out in the woods.

> (JOHN *looks like he might become sick during the following.*)

JOHN. Good.

CARMINE. Two in the heart, two in the head.

JOHN. Fine.

CARMINE. I mean there was blood. Lots of blood. But none of it's on the truck.

(JOHN *turns away and covers his mouth.* PHIL *prepares a stomach powder for* JOHN *and serves it to him.*)

There was this ditch nearby. I rolled him into that. They won't find what's left of him until the spring and by then his body will be all...

JOHN. *(interrupts)* Okay!

CARMINE. Huh?

JOHN. That's enough!

ANGELINA. You okay, John?

JOHN. Yeah, I'm... yeah...Every time I hear about blood or...I'm okay...

(JOHN *takes some deep breaths to recover, then forces a smile.*)

Joey, you going to Jersey tomorrow?

JOEY. Yeah, my brother's house. I'm taking my mother.

JOHN. I love your mother. Lovely woman. I just dropped by to say merry Christmas to her, she gives me three cases of Tennessee whiskey! Can you believe that?

CARMINE. How many cases?

JOHN. Three. The woman knows how to show respect.

JOEY. No!

JOHN. I swear. Very generous woman. Very generous. I love your mother, Joey.

JOEY. She loves you too, John.

JOHN. Jersey, huh?

(JOHN *takes out a huge wad of bills, peels off a few and hands them to* JOEY.)

This is for your brother's kids. Tell them it's from their Uncle John.

JOEY. I will. And thank you, John. My brother and his family thank you. Mille grazie.

JOHN. And I got a little Christmas gift for you.

(*to* **ANGELINA**)

Give 'em the thing.

ANGELINA. Hold on.

JOHN. Give 'em the thing!

(**ANGELINA** *struggles with the envelopes.*)

ANGELINA. I'm lookin'! Okay?

JOHN. Oh, come on!

ANGELINA. Wait!

(*They both lose control and scream at each other.*)

JOHN. Oh, come on, for Christ's sake! How long does it take! I asked you to do one thing for me! One thing! You can't even do that! Hand out some fuckin' envelopes! How difficult can that be! Look at you! Look at you! A fuckin' monkey could do this better! A fuckin' monkey! I say "Here, hold these envelopes and say the thing for me" and you can't even do that! You're helpless! One simple thing and you fuck it up! A monkey could do this!

ANGELINA. Don't start with me, John! Don't start! I'm in no mood! Aw, go to hell! You got a million fuckin' envelopes here! Who the hell can read your writing? Who the hell can read this scribble? They're not even in alphabetical order! Fuck you, John! Fuck you! Blow it out your ass! There's a thousand envelopes here and half of them are made out to someone named "Tony!" Get cancer and die! You smell like a monkey! And you write like one, too!

(**ANGELINA** *finds the right envelope then hands it to* **JOEY**.)

Here!

(*calmly*)

John Esposito wishes you a very merry Christmas and a New Year that is both healthy and prosperous.

JOEY. Thank you, John. Thank you very, very much.

JOHN. *(shrugs)* What the fuck. It's Christmas. We gotta celebrate the birth of Jesus H. Christ with love.

(**JOHN** *sits at a table where he's joined by* **CARMINE** *and* **JOEY.**)

ANGELINA. What do you want me to do now, John?

JOHN. Go sit down. Keep yourself busy or somethin'. Go do your little puzzle books or whatever it is you do.

ANGELINA. They're not puzzle books.

JOHN. Whatever!

ANGELINA. I'm increasing my word power in ninety days.

JOHN. Who the fuck cares!

ANGELINA. It wouldn't kill you to increase *your* word power a little.

JOHN. Get sick and die, will yuh!

ANGELINA. "Fuckin' A" is all I ever hear from you. "John, you having the steak?" "Fuckin' A!" "John, lookit the sunset!" "Fuckin' A!" "Fuckin' A! Fuckin' A! Fuckin' A!" Not everything in life is "Fuckin' A!" John.

JOHN. Fuckin' A shut *up*!

ANGELINA. John, you are so arbitrary it ain't even funny!

JOHN. Crazy bitch.

(**ANGELINA** *sits at another table, opens a paperback and studies it silently.*)

JOEY. You're out late tonight, John.

JOHN. It's Christmas. There's lots of Christmas-y stuff to do. Gifts to buy, parties to go to, cops to pay off.

(then)

Phil…

(**JOHN** *holds his thumb and index finger an inch apart indicating he'd like a drink.*)

PHIL. Comin' up.

(**PHIL** *pours a better brand of scotch into a coffee cup.*)

JOHN. Then, in the middle of all this Christmas shit, Vincent calls a meeting tonight.

JOEY. Vincent?

CARMINE. On Christmas Eve?

JOHN. Fuckin' A!

CARMINE. Someone else goin' to South Carolina?

JOHN. Not this time. This time the meeting was business. Important business. Vincent called in all the heads of the family. You know what's comin' to Queens this summer.

JOEY. Of course.

CARMINE. Everyone knows.

JOEY. The World's Fair.

JOHN. That's right. It's a fair but it's for the whole world.

JOEY. I like the way you explain that, John.

CARMINE. It's a fair…

JOEY. But it's for the whole world.

CARMINE. Yeah.

JOEY. Nice.

CARMINE. I like that.

JOEY. Sounds good.

JOHN. Vincent carved up the World's Fair tonight and we got ourselves one helluva slice. Here's how it breaks down: hookers, that's all gonna be Tony the Wheel.

JOEY. That's all he does.

CARMINE. Nothin' else.

JOEY. He's great with hookers.

CARMINE. He'll do great.

JOHN. Let's hope so because there's people comin' here from all over the world.

JOEY. So?

JOHN. So these girls, they gotta fuck in different languages.

JOEY/CARMINE. Yeah…Right…Of course…Gotta…

JOEY. Never thought of that.

JOHN. Gamblin' and loan sharkin' goes to Pauley.

JOEY. Pauley's very good at that.

CARMINE. Very good.

JOHN. That's why he got picked. Garbage is Freddy Fat Ass.

JOEY. He can kiss my balls.

CARMINE. Dipshit.

JOEY. Asshole.

CARMINE. Douchebag.

JOEY. Fuckhead.

CARMINE. Jerkoff.

JOHN. He can have it. And most of the construction goes to the Rosatto Brothers. But the concrete, that's ours.

JOEY. All right!

CARMINE. Yeah!

JOHN. And we also get all of the food service, linens, parking, and souvenirs.

JOEY. Woa!

CARMINE. Marrone! We're gettin' all that?

JOHN. Yeah.

JOEY. A World's Fair.

JOHN. It's a fair but it's for the whole world.

(**PHIL** *crosses to* **JOHN** *and serves him his scotch.*)

PHIL. Doesn't the city award these things to the lowest bidder? You know, with, what is it, sealed bids, something like that?

JOHN. They do. But when they open them sealed bids...

JOEY. Uh huh.

JOHN. Something tells me we're gonna get all kinds of lucky and win.

(*They all share a menacing chuckle.*)

JOEY. Good.

CARMINE. Yeah.

PHIL. I don't know why I bothered to ask.

JOHN. *(mock surprise)* "Ooo! I get all the food and restaurants? Wadda surprise!"

(then)

Vincent says this fair will draw more than twenty million people.

JOEY. Marrone!

PHIL. Damn!

CARMINE. Mama mia! Will Queens even *hold* twenty million people?

JOHN. They're not all comin' on the same day, you fuckin' idiot! It's spread out over two summers!

CARMINE. Oh. Well, that's what I mean.

JOHN. Vincent is already buyin' up some of the slums around here to turn it into parking.

PHIL. There go my friends.

JOHN. It's not personal, Phil. It's progress.

PHIL. Every time a colored man moves away it's progress.

(PHIL crosses back behind the counter.)

JOHN. *(re PHIL)* Love that guy.

JOEY. Man, we've been waiting on this World's Fair thing for a long time.

CARMINE. Long time now.

JOHN. Well, it'll be here before you know it. This summer Queens will be neck deep in people from all over the world. Krauts, Frogs, Spics, Micks, Beaners, Polacks, Camel Jockeys, Ricans, Ruskies, Hayseeds, Bohunks, Towelheads, Canucks, Spades, Limeys, Gooks, Chinks, Japs, Italians…

CARMINE. Foreign scum. Except for the Italians.

JOHN. Except for them. Everyone else…

CARMINE. Foreign scum.

JOHN. Foreign scum with money. They're gonna buy food, soda, beer, candy…

JOEY. You bet.

JOHN. That's gonna be us. They might be foreign scum but they're gonna get hungry.

JOEY. You bet!

CARMINE. And how!

JOHN. They want to buy a hotdog but it costs a dollar!

JOEY. A buck twenty-five!

CARMINE. A buck and a half!

JOHN. What do they do? Find City Hall, cry to the mayor?

(*mocking*)

"Ooo! The man wants too much money for a hotdog!"

CARMINE. Fuck no! They're gonna *pay* it!

JOHN. Foreign scum.

CARMINE. Then they leave New York pissed off because it was too fuckin' expensive.

JOHN. And they never come back!

CARMINE. Who gives a fuck! We got their money!

JOHN. Exactly! "Go on! Get outta here! Yuh Limey-Chink-Jap foreign scum!"

(**CARMINE** *raises his coffee cup.*)

CARMINE. To foreign scum.

JOEY. Foreign scum.

JOHN. Foreign scum.

(*They toast and drink.*)

Hey, Phil. Pour yourself a drink, put it on my tab.

(**PHIL** *pours himself a drink.*)

PHIL. Sure thing. What're we drinkin' to?

JOHN. Foreign scum.

PHIL. Sounds good to me.

(**ANGELINA** *rises and begins to cross to the ladies room.*)

JOHN. Hey! Where you goin'?

ANGELINA. I'm going to the bathroom, John! Do I gotta ask permission?

JOHN. I'm just askin'!

ANGELINA. Well, where else would I be goin'!

JOHN. I don't know where the fuck you're goin'! I'm just askin'!

ANGELINA. I'm goin' to do the cha-cha with Trini Lopez, okay!

JOHN. I'm just askin'!

ANGELINA. Well, I'm gonna go to the bathroom. Is that all right with you?

JOHN. I was just worried about you, is all.

(They both lose control and scream at each other.)

ANGELINA. All day long you don't say two fuckin' words to me now you're worried about me?! You are so full of shit! I got no life with you around! No life! I can't even go pee without you sayin' somethin' about it! I'm gonna pee! Is that all right? Is it all right I go to the God damn bathroom? My dog has a better life than me! My dog! "Where you goin'? When you comin' back?" You drive me fuckin' crazy, John! I can't take it no more! Fuck you, John!

JOHN. Aw, Jesus! No one can even talk to you anymore! No one! I say the slightest thing you fly off the handle! Stop! Just stop! You demean yourself when you talk like that! Totally demean! Just makin' yourself lower if that's possible! Street trash! From the gutter! Just stop! Will you! The mouth on you! And on Christmas Eve! No respect for Christ or his mother or the Pope or nothin'! Crazy bitch! Shut up, will ya! Just shut the fuck up!

ANGELINA. You're worried about me going to the bathroom? John, you are so ambiguous it ain't funny.

*(**ANGELINA** shoots **JOHN** a snooty look then exits to the ladies room.)*

JOHN. Crazy bitch.

CARMINE. Anyway…

JOEY. John, you know we'd do anything for you. Give up our lives if we had to.

CARMINE. Take a bullet.

JOEY. Both of us.

CARMINE. Any time.

JOEY. Day or night.

CARMINE. You call me up, three in the morning. You say "Hey, I need you to take a bullet for me." I'm there.

JOEY. Me, too.

(JOHN slowly begins to get sick to his stomach again. PHIL begins to prepare a stomach powder for JOHN but stops.)

CARMINE. Take a bullet.

JOEY. In the heart.

CARMINE. The stomach.

JOEY. Right in the head, John. I would take a bullet in the head.

CARMINE. In the *face.*

JOEY. Me, too. Right in the face. Closed casket, I wouldn't give a shit.

CARMINE. I'd take a dozen bullets for you, John. Or a knife. A knife right in the gut!

JOHN. *(interrupts)* Okay! I get it! I get it! Thank you!

CARMINE. We just want you to know how we feel about you.

JOHN. I know. You're both good boys.

JOEY. Carmine and me, we know you got guys to cover construction and food. I mean, that's your thing. That's all in place. But there's one thing you don't have covered and Carmine and me, we'd like a shot at it. We wanna show you what we can do. Besides fillin' vending machines.

CARMINE. And runnin' cigs up from South Carolina.

JOHN. What're you thinkin'?

JOEY. Souvenirs.

JOHN. Souvenirs?

JOEY. We'd like to run that for you. With your permission.

CARMINE. And your blessing.

JOEY. I know a guy. He does the souvenirs for the Statue of Liberty, the Empire State Building. They knock out this souvenir crap in Hong Kong for pennies, sell it for two, three dollars. We could put the whole thing together for you, John. But only with your permission.

CARMINE. And your blessing.

JOEY. Tutto rispetto, John.

CARMINE. Tutto rispetto.

(They take turns kissing JOHN's pinky ring.)

JOHN. One thing I always liked about you two; you know how to show proper respect.

CARMINE. You deserve it, John.

JOEY. You've been very generous with us.

CARMINE. And our families.

JOEY. My mother thinks you're a saint.

CARMINE. Mine, too.

JOEY. My mother has your picture hanging in her dining room. Right between the Pope and Frank Sinatra.

JOHN. Souvenirs.

JOEY. But only with your permission.

CARMINE. And your blessing.

JOHN. Twenty million people. If each one spends two bucks on a souvenir.

(JOHN takes out his pad and pencil and does the math.)

Carry the zero… zero, zero… That's forty million. Big step.

CARMINE. We're ready, John.

JOEY. We want to do good for the family.

(ANGELINA peeks out from the ladies room. She sees JOHN is talking with JOEY and CARMINE and ducks back in.)

JOHN. I tell you what.

    (thinks, then)

    You two put some sample stuff together. Whatever it is you want to sell. Put it together, show me.

CARMINE. All right!

JOEY. Yeah!

JOHN. I'm not sayin' you got it yet, but if I like what I see, the job is yours.

CARMINE. Oh, man!

JOEY. Yes!

JOHN. *(calling)* Angelina! Let's go!

ANGELINA. *(offstage)* I'm not ready!

JOHN. Well, c'mon!

JOEY. I'll call this souvenir guy right away.

CARMINE. We'll show you some really good stuff.

JOHN. I'm going to Florida tomorrow for nine, ten days so not this Friday but the Friday after, I want to meet with you guys, see what you come up with.

CARMINE. Not this Friday.

JOHN. But the Friday after.

CARMINE. We'll be ready.

JOHN. *(calling)* Angelina!

ANGELINA. *(offstage)* What!

JOHN. I gotta go!

ANGELINA. *(offstage)* I need more time!

JOHN. Bitch.

    (then)

    We're on the inside with this thing. New York is ours. Queens is ours. The World's Fair is ours.

CARMINE. We won't call it the 1964 World's Fair.

JOEY. We'll call it John Esposito's World's Fair.

JOHN. I like that. That's nice. Remember, not this Friday.

JOEY. But the Friday after.

JOHN. After New Year's.

> (**JOHN** *crosses to the ladies' room and opens the door a few inches.*)

Are you ready or not!

ANGELINA. *(offstage)* I'm not! God, stop rushing me!

JOHN. I gotta go!

ANGELINA. *(offstage)* I'm so impressed!

JOHN. How much longer!

ANGELINA. *(offstage)* It's gonna be a while.

JOHN. It's late, I gotta get home. Joey, run Angelina back to Howard Beach for me?

JOEY. Done. Put it out of your mind. She's already home. Safe and sound.

JOHN. Phil, if anyone calls and asks if I was with Angelina…

PHIL. Never saw her.

JOHN. Excellent.

PHIL. I didn't even see you.

JOHN. Even better.

JOEY. Did you see me and Carmine?

PHIL. I'm sorry, have we met?

> (**JOEY** *smiles.* **JOHN** *hands* **PHIL** *an envelope.*)

JOHN. Merry Christmas.

PHIL. Oh, thank you, John. Thank you very much. That's very kind of you. Thank you.

JOHN. What the fuck. It's Christmas for colored people, too.

> (**JOHN** *opens the ladies' room door a crack.*)

I'm goin'.

ANGELINA. *(offstage)* You're what?

JOHN. I gotta go now. Besides, you live the other way.

ANGELINA. *(offstage)* What?

JOHN. You live in Howard Beach, I'm in Long Island!

ANGELINA. *(offstage)* What's this, a geography lesson?

JOHN. Joey's takin' you home! I gotta go!

ANGELINA. *(offstage)* Then go!

JOHN. I gotta!

ANGELINA. *(offstage)* Then *go!*

JOHN. What?

ANGELINA. *(offstage)* Then *go!*

JOHN. Okay.

> *(beat)*

> Merry Christmas.

ANGELINA. *(offstage)* Yeah, and a New Year that is both healthy and prosperous!

JOHN. Don't start with me!

ANGELINA. *(offstage)* Fuck you! This is the way we celebrate Christmas Eve together? You sayin' goodbye to me while I'm in the ladies room?! Eat shit and die, John! Sunovabitch! A gold wristwatch and a good-bye while I'm on the toilet! What a Christmas to remember! No class! No class at all! Merry Christmas, John! And let me wish you a new year that is both healthy and prosperous you two face bastard!

JOHN. Don't start with me again! I'm in no mood for your shit! Understand! No mood! The mouth on you! Ignorance! You only show your ignorance! Low class! Low class! Please! You only lower yourself! Trash! Like your family! Low class, ignorant trash! Money grubbing, low class bitch! You're nothin'! Hear me! Nothin'! Sacrilegious bitch! You'll rot in hell for half the crap you say! Rot in hell!

> Crazy bitch.

> *(to JOEY and CARMINE)*

> I gotta go.

> *(JOHN closes the door then turns to JOEY and CARMINE and sighs.)*

JOEY. You can't help it.

CARMINE. You gotta go.

JOHN. I do.

JOEY. She'll be all right.

> (**JOHN** *prepares to leave.*)
>
> Goodbye, John.

CARMINE. Merry Christmas.

JOEY. Yeah, Merry Christmas.

CARMINE. Happy New Year.

JOEY. Happy New Year, John.

CARMINE. God bless you, John.

JOEY. Our best to your family.

CARMINE. Safe trip to Florida.

JOEY. Yeah, have a safe trip.

CARMINE. Night.

JOHN. Remember, it's a fair…

JOEY/CARMINE/JOHN. But it's for the whole world.

> (**JOHN** *exits. The instant the door closes* **JOEY** *and* **CARMINE** *hug and back slap.*)

JOEY. All right!

CARMINE. Yeah!

JOEY. We got it!

CARMINE. Big time!

> (*As* **JOEY** *and* **CARMINE** *continue to talk* **ANGELINA** *peeks out from the ladies' room then goes back inside.*)

JOEY. Souvenirs!

CARMINE. They're gonna be ours!

JOEY. Every last one of 'em!

CARMINE. We're gonna be rich.

JOEY. You bet. This guy who makes souvenirs. I'll call him tomorrow. Get him started. I feel good about this.

CARMINE. Me, too. Maybe…

JOEY. Maybe what?

CARMINE. Maybe I've seen my last trip for cigarettes.

JOEY. Maybe I've seen my last jukebox.

CARMINE. I can't take another trip to South Carolina. I know three guys named Bubba.

JOEY. Our lives are gonna change plenty. And this all happened tonight.

CARMINE. On Christmas Eve.

JOEY. On Christmas Eve.

CARMINE. Can't no one ever tell me good shit don't happen on Christmas.

(suddenly)

Ooo! That reminds me!

*(**CARMINE** hands **JOEY** an eight track tape.)*

That's for you.

JOEY. You bought me something?

CARMINE. I didn't really "buy" it. The guy at Sam Goody's was such a prick I decided to lift a dozen eight tracks.

JOEY. Love these eight tracks!

(reads label)

"Vic Damone Sings Sinatra!" Hey, c'mon!

CARMINE. You like?

JOEY. Love this! Hey, I'm gonna play this on my way home. Merry Christmas, Carmine.

CARMINE. Merry friggin' Christmas to you, too. I love you like you was my brother, Joey.

JOEY. Same here, Carmine.

(They hug.)

CARMINE. I especially love you…

JOEY. Yeah?

CARMINE. *(teasing)* When you dance alone!

*(**CARMINE** does a mock dance and the two laugh.)*

Woo! Woo! Merry Christmas, kid.

JOEY. You, too. Merry Christmas.

(CARMINE exits. JOEY goes back to servicing the jukebox.)

You hear that, Phil?

PHIL. Huh?

JOEY. Me and Carmine. We might do all the souvenirs for the World's Fair.

PHIL. I didn't hear nothin'.

(PHIL exits to the back as JOEY smiles and shakes his head. A beat then ANGELINA enters from the ladies' room.)

ANGELINA. Did he go?

JOEY. John?

ANGELINA. Uh huh.

JOEY. Yeah, he left.

ANGELINA. Where's the other guy?

JOEY. Carmine. He just left, too.

ANGELINA. Man, I can really empty a joint, can't I?

JOEY. It's nothin' to do with you. They had to get home.

ANGELINA. Yeah.

JOEY. I'll run you back to Howard Beach as soon as I'm done.

ANGELINA. No rush.

(She watches him finish up his work with the jukebox for a few beats.)

That what you do?

JOEY. Hmm?

ANGELINA. For John. That what you do?

JOEY. Long time. But I might be movin' up in the family. Makin' my move. You watch. But for now...

(JOEY jingles pocket change.)

"Joey Nickels." Jukeboxes, cigarette and vending machines.

ANGELINA. That's how you got your name?

JOEY. It's how all of us get our name. All of us who work for John, it's kinda tribal.

ANGELINA. What's that mean?

JOEY. Tribal. In some ways we're a lot like Indians. If you do a particular thing or there's something that's special about you, that thing becomes part of your name.

ANGELINA. Who told you that?

JOEY. Tony the Asshole.

(**ANGELINA** *breaks out laughing, then* **JOEY.**)

ANGELINA. Tony the…Wadda pisser!

JOEY. Okay, there's no such guy. But you ever meet Frankie Four Aces?

ANGELINA. Sure.

JOEY. The story goes he was in a poker game, got four aces.

ANGELINA. Frankie Four Aces.

JOEY. Danny Cadillac.

ANGELINA. Always drives a Cadillac?

JOEY. Went to Florida to see his mother. The rental car joint was out of Caddies. Got on a plane and went back home.

ANGELINA. Wow.

JOEY. Won't even *ride* in another car. Carmine the Camel.

ANGELINA. The guy who just left.

JOEY. Makes two runs a week down to South Carolina for cigarettes. You ask him for a cigarette.

ANGELINA. It's going to be a Camel.

JOEY. Always.

ANGELINA. And you're Joey Nickels.

JOEY. My pockets, the trunk of my car, where I live, I got dozens of jars full of nickels.

ANGELINA. What you do becomes your name.

JOEY. Like Indians.

ANGELINA. Right. Like Indians.

(*She watches him for several more beats.*)

Where'd you learn that?

JOEY. Learn what?

ANGELINA. The tribal thing, Indians.

JOEY. I read.

ANGELINA. Read what?

JOEY. Books.

ANGELINA. What kind?

JOEY. Ones that teach me stuff.

ANGELINA. I read, too. I bought a book. I'm reading it right now.

JOEY. What's it called?

ANGELINA. "Increase Your Word Power in Ninety Days" by Random House.

JOEY. How's that comin'?

ANGELINA. I dunno, this is only the third day. I'm still in the "A's."

JOEY. Ah.

ANGELINA. But I think it'll do me some good.

JOEY. Yeah. I heard you before. With John. What'd you call him again?

ANGELINA. Ambiguous.

JOEY. Ambiguous.

ANGELINA. Like that?

JOEY. I love it and I don't even know what it means.

ANGELINA. It means you're not clear, you're not for sure. You're one way and the other at the same time.

JOEY. Woa. Then that's a real put down.

ANGELINA. Good. I skipped ahead in the book and peeked at some other words. Next time I see John I'm going to call him fallacious.

JOEY. Fa what?

ANGELINA. Fallacious.

JOEY. Isn't that a sex thing? Something people do in bed?

ANGELINA. No. Fallacious means to be false or misleading.

JOEY. Oh, man. John's gonna be mad if he ever figures out what you're sayin'.

ANGELINA. He won't. He's too lazy and stupid to buy a dictionary. Even if he did he wouldn't know how to spell half of what I'm going to call him.

(beat)

So what's a smart guy like you doing with John?

JOEY. I could ask you the same thing.

ANGELINA. Money.

JOEY. That's my answer, too.

ANGELINA. My mother, she's got a heart thing. It's expensive as hell. I don't want her in some city hospital so…

JOEY. I gotcha.

ANGELINA. So it works out, except for the part where I've got to stay home all the time and answer the phone on the first ring because that's the way John likes it. So I read. Book by book, I'm going to study myself into being smarter. You watch. I'll do it. I'll get smarter. Real smart.

JOEY. Sometimes I wish I was smarter. But then I tell myself at least I'm not one of the DeMarcos.

ANGELINA. Who's that?

JOEY. We lived next door to the DeMarcos when I was a kid. Now my family wasn't educated and stuff but the DeMarcos, they were the stupidest five people God ever made. I think they were sharin' a brain. Their idea of conversation was to grunt and point. Jesus Christ, they got through life on, I dunno, maybe fifty words. They used to fix cars in the driveway every weekend. The father would crawl under the car and you'd hear him tell his kids, "Gimme the thing! The thing!" And the kids would hand him a hammer. And he'd go, "No, no, the thing! The thing!" And the kids would hand him a screw driver. And he'd get pissed off and yell, "Not that thing, the thing! The thing!" And they'd ask him, "What thing? The big thing or the little thing?" And he'd answer them! "Not the big thing or the little thing! The medium thing!" There was no hope for these people! The guy owns four thousand tools and he's got the same name for all of them, "The thing!" What he usually wanted was...

(slowly)

...a crescent head wrench...

(then)

but he didn't call it that. He called it, "The thing!"

(The two become lost in each other's eyes.)

Simple things become difficult when you don't know how to say what it is you want.

ANGELINA. You know what you want?

JOEY. Always.

*(**ANGELINA** is the first to snap out of the gaze.)*

ANGELINA. I'll remember to tell that to John when I see him tomorrow.

JOEY. You won't see John tomorrow.

ANGELINA. Oh, right, it's Christmas. Whatever, the day after tomorrow.

JOEY. Not even then. He's headed to Florida for nine, ten days.

(beat)

He didn't tell you?

ANGELINA. No.

(sarcastic)

It must've skipped his mind. He's comin' back after New Years?

JOEY. Not this Friday but the Friday after.

ANGELINA. Another New Year's Eve.

JOEY. And what? You got nothin' to do?

ANGELINA. Just like last year.

JOEY. You did nothin' last year?

ANGELINA. Oh, I did plenty. I did my nails and watched the ball drop in Times Square on television.

JOEY. You wanna do somethin'?

ANGELINA. What?

JOEY. I'm not doin' anything New Year's Eve. Wanna hook up, do somethin'?

ANGELINA. If John found out he'd kill you.

JOEY. Well, John ain't gonna find out unless you love him so much you gotta go tell him.

ANGELINA. What is it? You looking for some cheap and easy sex so you figure you'll buy John's goumada a hamburger then get laid?

JOEY. Hey, c'mon, listen this isn't about sex. This is about havin' a good time on New Year's Eve, that's all. And when I take a woman out I don't take her for no hamburger. I do it right. I put on a suit and tie, I clean the car, I pick her up and I don't blow the horn, I ring her bell, then I take her anywhere she says she wants to go. That's what you do when you take a woman out. You take her where she wants to go. Anywhere.

ANGELINA. Anywhere?

JOEY. Anywhere you want. The Copa has Tony Bennett, we can go to the Waldorf, listen to Guy Lombardo, Times Square. You name it.

ANGELINA. Roseland.

JOEY. What?

ANGELINA. I want to go to Roseland. They got three orchestras. All night long. Non stop.

JOEY. Roseland.

ANGELINA. Yeah. Dancing.

JOEY. You really want to do that?

ANGELINA. Yeah!

JOEY. It's gonna be so crowded and you don't know. I could be a terrible dancer.

ANGELINA. But you're not. I heard John say you're a good dancer. Real good. He says you were all up in the Catskills one weekend, and you won a dance contest with some woman you just pulled out of the crowd.

JOEY. Oh, that. That was...

ANGELINA. He says you and this woman did such a good job her husband got all kinds of jealous. Carmine had to beat him up.

JOEY. Oh, that. Yeah, well, Carmine's always beating people up.

ANGELINA. What's the deal? You don't want to go dancing with me?

JOEY. No, no. It's just that...

ANGELINA. What?

JOEY. I know a lotta people at Roseland. And I take my dancin' very serious. My mother and father were ballroom dancers. I mean they competed and stuff. So did I. I used to teach ballroom in the Poconos. Our house is wall to wall trophies.

ANGELINA. And what? You think I'm gonna cramp your style? Hurt your rep?

JOEY. No. No. It's just that a lotta women have trouble keepin' up.

ANGELINA. Listen, I was born to dance. My mother ran a dance studio in our basement. Before she met my father she was a goddamn Rockette.

JOEY. So?

ANGELINA. So there ain't nothin' you can do on a dance floor I can't keep up with.

JOEY. Angelina, if I take you to Roseland you'll wind up watching me dance with some other woman who knows how.

ANGELINA. That other woman...

JOEY. Yeah?

ANGELINA. Is me.

JOEY. Think so?

ANGELINA. Know so.

JOEY. Let's see.

ANGELINA. Your funeral. Got a nickel?

JOEY. It's my last name.

(**JOEY** *hands* **ANGELINA** *a nickel. She puts it in the juke box and surveys the selection.*)

ANGELINA. Some rock and roll?

JOEY. That's for cowards and amateurs.

ANGELINA. Something that takes some style?

JOEY. If you got any.

(**ANGELINA** *smiles then pushes a button on the juke box. She turns to face* **JOEY**, *tilts her head back and takes the pose of a professional ballroom dancer.* **JOEY**, *not about to be outdone, does the same. A slow, romantic ballad like "Crying" or "Unforgettable" begins to play.)**

(*The song, slow, sultry and full of love unfulfilled seems to fit the moment perfectly.* **ANGELINA** *makes the first move and* **JOEY** *is right with her. They dance separately, mirror images of each other, not yet touching and the distance between them is exquisite.*)

(*During the song the lights will dim until* **JOEY** *and* **ANGELINA** *are bathed in a warm spotlight. A mirrored ball will send specks of starlight floating across the walls.*)

(**ANGELINA** *spins into* **JOEY**'*s arms and they sweep across the floor effortlessly, as though they have done this dance a thousand times. Their dance is pure splendor and romance as* **JOEY** *dips and twirls* **ANGELINA** *with ease.*)

(*She spins out of his arms then back into a tight embrace. The dance is nothing less than a timeless expression of grace and intimacy.*)

(*The lights slowly fade to black.*)

End Act One

---

*Please see Music Use Note on page 3.

ACT TWO

Scene One

*(It is nine days later. The lights come up to reveal **JOEY** and **CARMINE** at a table with **LENNY GREEN**. **LENNY** is a pleasant, timid and overweight middle-aged man. Potential souvenirs for the upcoming World's Fair are scattered on the table along with paperwork and order pads.)*

*(**PHIL** hunches over the counter reading a newspaper as always.)*

LENNY. Okay. Next on our list. Souvenir spoons.

*(**JOEY** and **CARMINE** examine a sample spoon.)*

JOEY. Lookit this. The handle has writing on it that says "1964 World's Fair." Hey, Phil you see this?

PHIL. I didn't see nothin'.

*(**JOEY** and **CARMINE** exchange a smile.)*

JOEY. Nice lookin' spoon.

CARMINE. And it's silver.

LENNY. Polished steel actually.

JOEY. We'll say it's silver.

CARMINE. Yeah. Fourteen karat silver.

LENNY. Ooo, we can't do that.

CARMINE. Why not?

LENNY. Because it's not silver. Not even silver plated.

CARMINE. So?

LENNY. So it's against the law.

CARMINE. What law is that? The You-Can't-Call-it-Silver-Law?

LENNY. But the government says you can't do that.

CARMINE. The government says a lotta stuff they really don't mean.

JOEY. We're going to say this is solid silver.

LENNY. And what are you going to do when people find out it's not solid silver?

CARMINE. You mean what are we gonna do when people get back to Swamp Dump, Florida? And the spoon turns green two years later? And they jump in their car and drive *back* to Queens? Back to the World's Fair? To complain?! But all they can find is two Puerto Ricans playin' handball? Because the World's Fair is fuckin' *gone?* Is that what we're supposed to worry about?

JOEY. We want little tags that say "solid silver."

CARMINE. Write that down. "Solid silver." Write it down!

(**LENNY** *writes it down as* **CARMINE** *takes* **JOEY** *aside.*)

Joey, c'mere. Know what I like about these little spoons?

JOEY. What?

CARMINE. They're little. I mean if a couple thousand of them got "lost" no one would know.

JOEY. Jesus, Carmine!

CARMINE. What!

JOEY. We don't even have this job yet and you're already figuring out ways to skim.

CARMINE. Hey, it never hurts to plan ahead. By the way, I put forty cases of cigarettes in your garage.

JOEY. Again!

CARMINE. Your mother wanted three cases for her trouble but I got her to take two.

JOEY. Hey, Carmine!

CARMINE. They'll be gone tomorrow. Swear to God!

JOEY. Next time I want you to ask me first. "Joey, can I put forty cases of cigs in your garage?" I want you to do that.

CARMINE. Why?

JOEY. So I can say "no."

(suddenly)

Shh! Careful, it's John!

CARMINE. I see 'im. I see 'im.

*(**JOHN ESPOSITO** enters followed by **ANGELINA**. Again he doesn't bother to hold the door for her. **JOEY** and **ANGELINA** exchange furtive glances then she crosses to a table where she sits and quietly studies her book.)*

John!

JOEY. Hey, John!

CARMINE. Back from Florida!

JOEY. How was it?

JOHN. Hot, humid, full of Jews and alligators.

CARMINE. Well, you look good, John.

JOEY. Well rested.

CARMINE. Got some nice color.

JOEY. Very nice.

CARMINE. Nice tan.

JOEY. When'd you get back?

JOHN. Yesterday. As soon as I heard the terrible news about Frankie Four Aces.

CARMINE. What a shame.

JOEY. A tragedy.

CARMINE. Right in front of his favorite seafood joint.

JOEY. And they whacked him goin' *in*. Not on his way out. That means he didn't even get to have dinner.

CARMINE. That's not right.

JOEY. Shot him eight times. Like a dog.

*(**JOHN** looks like he might become sick during the following. **PHIL** prepares a stomach powder for **JOHN**.)*

CARMINE. And he took one in the eye which means a closed casket.

JOEY. Who shoots someone in the eye?

CARMINE. My mother says you don't get to see the face of God if they shoot you in the eye.

JOEY. Well, maybe if they shoot you in *both* eyes.

CARMINE. Right. Frankie can still see God with his good eye.

JOEY. Wait, what are we talkin' here? God can fix the bad eye.

CARMINE. Well, if He can fix one eye He can fix 'em both.

JOEY. If you were shot in both eyes.

CARMINE. My mother is so fuckin' stupid! "Can't see the face of God?"

JOEY. God'll fix it!

CARMINE. He can fix anything!

JOEY. Even if you got a million bullets in you!

JOHN. Stop!

CARMINE. Oh. Sorry, John.

JOHN. It's okay. I just…I'm…I'm okay…

CARMINE. My fault.

ANGELINA. You want a bucket or something, John?

JOHN. Naw, naw. I'm all right.

(*then*)

Maybe.

(*then*)

False alarm. I'm okay.

ANGELINA. You sure?

JOHN. Yeah.

ANGELINA. What do you want me to do now, John?

JOHN. Just go sit. Do whatever the fuck it is you do.

(**ANGELINA** *crosses to a table and sits.*)

The piece of shit who did this to Frankie. The person who has slapped the face of our family. We will hunt him down like a dog. We'll find this cocksucker and make him *beg* for death.

JOEY. Beg for death.

CARMINE. Beg for death.

JOHN. Beg for death.

CARMINE. *Beg* for death.

> (**CARMINE**, **JOEY** *and* **JOHN** *all realize* **LENNY** *has been staring at them with a look of absolute amazement. All eyes slowly turn to* **LENNY**.)

JOHN. Who's the fat guy?

CARMINE. Oh, him.

JOEY. This is Lenny. He's the souvenir guy I was tellin' you about.

CARMINE. We've been taking care of that. Just like you said.

JOEY. I mean, we haven't ordered anything. We just put together some samples.

CARMINE. Just like you said.

JOHN. Samples, huh? For the New York World's Fair?

JOEY. It's a fair…

CARMINE. But it's for the whole world.

JOHN. Okay, let's see what you got.

CARMINE. Really?

JOHN. Yeah.

JOEY. Right now?

JOHN. No, a million years from now! Of course right now. C'mon, I'm standin' right here, I wanna see. Angelina!

ANGELINA. What!

JOHN. C'mere!

ANGELINA. What for?

JOHN. I want you to see this stuff.

ANGELINA. What stuff?

JOHN. This stuff over here! C'mon! I need a woman's opinion. It'll only take a second.

ANGELINA. I just sat down.

JOHN. Well now I'm asking you to get up.

ANGELINA. Jesus Christ, make up your mind. Sit down, stand up, go here, go there! Like I'm some kinda dog! I'm not a dog, John! I'm a human being with feelings an' stuff! Understand! Not a dog! Human being! If you wanted me over there you should've said "Hey, stay here for a minute. I want you to see somethin'." But no! You tell me to come over here, two seconds later you want me to go over there! This shit is drivin' me nuts, John! Drivin' me nuts! Eat shit and die!

JOHN. Aw, for Christ's sake I'm askin' you nice! Do me one little favor! One little thing! Is this too much to ask? Get up and walk ten feet over here! I didn't know they had anything over there until you came over here. Do you have to? Do you have to! Please! Stop! Would you please! Is it too much to ask? There's no talking to you! Get up! Please? C'mon, I'm askin' you nice. Do this one thing for me, 'kay? C'mon, act like a human being just this once! Please? C'mon...

(as ANGELINA crosses to JOHN.)

ANGELINA. Asshole.

JOHN. *(sotto to JOEY and CARMINE)* Women see stuff different from men. They're all fucked up.

(to ANGELINA)

Take a look with me. This is souvenir stuff for the World's Fair.

ANGELINA. World's Fair?

JOHN. Yeah. It's a fair but it's for the whole world.

(to LENNY)

Go 'head.

LENNY. Hmm?

CARMINE. Show him.

(no response.)

Show John what you got!

LENNY. *(snapping out of it)* Oh, I'm sorry.

(then)

I uh…let's see… I've been showing samples here… I was about to show the World's Fair T-shirt.

*(**LENNY** holds up a Worlds Fair T-shirt.)*

CARMINE. Very colorful.

LENNY. And these days, the new trend in T-shirts is "one size fits all."

CARMINE. One sit fits all, huh?

JOHN. They oughta call it "one size fits all except *you*." Listen, Chunky. If I decide to do business with you, don't try and gimme this "one size fits all" bullshit. I want fat people to buy T-shirts, too.

JOEY. We'll sell 'em for what?

CARMINE. Five bucks.

JOHN. Yeah, five bucks. I like that. Round numbers. Five bucks.

LENNY. No one ever charges more than two dollars.

JOEY. We're chargin' five.

LENNY. Well go ahead, but you'll get murdered by your competition.

*(**JOHN**, **JOEY**, and **CARMINE** break out laughing.)*

What?

(beat)

What!

JOHN. Could you say that again?

LENNY. Say what?

CARMINE. The last part.

LENNY. You'll get murdered by your competition?

(They break out laughing again.)

CARMINE. "Murdered."

JOEY. I know! I know!

JOHN. You gotta love that!

CARMINE. You gotta!

JOHN. Competition!

CARMINE. That is so cute!

JOHN. Lenny, is it?

LENNY. Yes.

JOHN. My friends and I, my associates, when we do business, we do it so well, we do it with so much heart and and and...enthusiasm that...we don't *have* any competition.

(**LENNY** *stares at* **JOHN**, **JOEY** *and* **CARMINE** *as things finally begin to make sense to him.*)

LENNY. Oh, my God.

JOHN. What?

LENNY. I think I understand.

CARMINE. You do?

LENNY. Yes, I get what you're saying.

JOEY. Good. Show John what else you got.

LENNY. Very well.

(**LENNY** *holds up various items and rattles them off quickly.*)

We have the New York World's Fair metal ashtray, ceramic ashtray, imitation gold bracelet.

JOEY. Pure gold.

LENNY. *(quick to cover)* How stupid of me. Of course it's pure gold.

(then)

The New York World's Fair license plate frame, playing cards, key ring, nite lite, coffee mug, the comb, the brush, the comb and brush set, nut dish, pickle dish, candy dish, toothbrush, pennant, thermometer, the poster, the Souvenir World's Fair Coca Cola cup...

ANGELINA. Don't you need permission from Coca Cola?

CARMINE. We asked them and they were delighted about the whole thing.

LENNY. World's Fair sun visor, baseball hat, beer stein, coasters, shot glasses, swizzle sticks, flash light, pen, pencil, pencil box, salt and pepper shakers, snow globe, paper weight, tie clip, cuff links, note pad, hair clip, lapel pin, rain bonnet, umbrella and the Pieta nite light.

(JOHN *stares stone faced at all the merchandise. No one can tell if he's pleased or not. After several long, silent beats.*)

JOHN. Is that everything?

CARMINE. Yeah.

JOEY. That's everything.

JOHN. Angelina.

ANGELINA. What?

JOHN. What do you think?

ANGELINA. You're asking me?

JOHN. Yeah, I'm asking you.

ANGELINA. My honest opinion?

JOHN. No, I want you to lie and make up a bunch of shit! Of course, your honest opinion!

ANGELINA. You want to know what I think?

JOHN. Yeah and don't hold back.

ANGELINA. I think if you don't order a million of each and every one of these things you're out of your goddamn mind, John. This stuff is unbelievable.

JOHN. You like it?

ANGELINA. I *love* it! It's gorgeous! All of it! If I was going to the World's Fair I'd want one of everything. All this stuff! Lookit this stuff! Just lookit! It's beautiful!

(ANGELINA *shakes a snow globe.*)

Look, it's snowing in Queens. These guys are smart, John. Not like the other gorillas who work for you. These two got brains.

CARMINE. Thank you.

JOEY. You're very kind.

CARMINE. Thank you very much.

ANGELINA. May I make one tiny suggestion?

LENNY. Of course.

ANGELINA. Potholders. My mother collects them. Everywhere I go, I get her a souvenir potholder.

JOEY. Potholder.

ANGELINA. She don't use the potholders. She hangs them over the stove in a special place. When she's makin' dinner she can look at her potholders and dream about all the places she's never been.

CARMINE. Great idea.

(to **LENNY***)*

Write it down.

LENNY. Huh?

CARMINE. Potholders! Write it down!

*(***LENNY*** writes it down.)*

JOHN. Angelina's right. This stuff is beautiful. I love this shit. It oughta sell like hotcakes. Angelina, thanks.

ANGELINA. You're welcome. I'm always glad to act in a supplementary manner.

*(***ANGELINA*** throws* **JOEY** *a secret smile then crosses back to her table where she sits and reads.)*

JOHN. This is terrific what you guys did. I'm pleased. Very, very pleased. I never expected to see so much.

CARMINE. We wanted to do a good job, John.

JOEY. Show you we're serious about all this.

JOHN. Well, you did. You did. Joey, call Tommy Two Tone. Tell him we're going ahead with this. Hold on...hold on...

(to **LENNY***)*

How long does it take for this crap to get here from Hong Kong?

LENNY. Two months.

JOHN. *(to* **JOEY***)* Tell him in two months we'll need warehouse space.

JOEY. You got it!

*(***JOEY*** crosses to the pay phone, closes the door and makes the call.)*

JOHN. Very nice, Carmine. You did good.

LENNY. Ooo, there's one more thing you haven't seen. And this will sell big! Everyone's going to want one of these!

*(***LENNY*** takes out a Frisbee with World's Fair artwork on it.)*

JOHN. What the fuck is that?

LENNY. It's new. It's called a Frisbee.

CARMINE. What the fuck is a Frisbee?

LENNY. It's a toy. Kids love them! Adults love them, too.

*(***CARMINE*** takes the Frisbee and bangs it on the table.)*

CARMINE. *(sarcastic)* Ooo, yeah! Great! Wadda great toy! I want one for Christmas!

*(***LENNY*** takes the Frisbee back.)*

LENNY. No, you throw it.

JOHN. Yeah, right. You throw it *away.*

LENNY. No, you throw it *to* someone. They catch it and they throw it back. Once you see it fly, it's amazing.

CARMINE. *(mocking)* Ooo, it flies!

JOHN. *(mocking)* I'm scared!

LENNY. At least take a minute to see how it goes. But not in here. There's not enough room.

JOHN. The parking lot?

LENNY. Yes, that'll be perfect.

*(***LENNY*** crosses to the door followed by **CARMINE** and **JOHN***.)*

I'm not an expert thrower or anything. But if you throw it right it can really zing.

JOHN. Ooo, it zings!

CARMINE. I don't know if I should zing. I'm Catholic! I'm savin' it for when I get married!

JOHN. Angelina, wanna see the Frisbee?

ANGELINA. Like I wanna get pregnant.

(*JOHN,* **CARMINE** *and* **LENNY** *exit.* **ANGELINA** *crosses to the jukebox, puts in a nickel but doesn't press a button. After a few beats* **JOEY** *hangs up the phone and exits the phone booth.*)

JOEY. Where'd they go?

ANGELINA. Outside for a minute.

JOEY. Oh, well…hiya.

ANGELINA. Hi.

JOEY. How you been?

ANGELINA. Okay.

(*beat*)

You?

JOEY. Keepin' busy. Jukeboxes to fill.

ANGELINA. Nickels to roll.

JOEY. Always.

ANGELINA. Joey Nickels.

JOEY. That's right.

ANGELINA. Like the Indians.

JOEY. Like the Indians. Thanks for doin' that. With the souvenirs. Saying what you did.

ANGELINA. I meant it. You worked hard, you should sell a lot of those, move up in the family.

JOEY. How you doin' with your book, increasing your word power?

ANGELINA. I'm up to the "r's"

JOEY. Good for you. Keep at it.

ANGELINA. I will. I'm totally committed to it.

JOEY. Well, good.

ANGELINA. I approach it with an absolute resolve.

JOEY. (*impressed*) Ooo, you are up to the "r's."

ANGELINA. You hear about Jimmy?

JOEY. Jimmy Two Tone? Yeah, I just got off the phone with him.

ANGELINA. He's getting married this spring to Tammy.

JOEY. Tammy DeLatura.

ANGELINA. Of course, after the wedding her name will be Tammy Two Tone.

(They share a smile.)

JOEY. It don't work like that.

ANGELINA. I guess not.

JOEY. Jimmy asked me to be an usher at his wedding.

ANGELINA. I'm going to be a bridesmaid.

JOEY. No kiddin'. Really?

ANGELINA. Yeah.

JOEY. Well, good. We'll both be there.

(ANGELINA pushes a button on the juke box and a romantic song like "Oh What A Night" begins to play.* She begins to dance slightly. It's all very dreamy and seductive. JOEY fights the urge to dance but eventually gives in while he keeps a watchful eye on the parking lot.)

ANGELINA. Maybe we could dance.

JOEY. At the wedding?

ANGELINA. Yeah.

JOEY. Uh…

ANGELINA. Just one?

JOEY. I don't think that would be such a good idea.

ANGELINA. Why not?

JOEY. People might talk. Get suspicious.

ANGELINA. If we're both in the bridal party and we *don't* dance…people might get even *more* suspicious. "What's goin' on with Joey and Angelina? They're dancin' with everyone but not with each other."

JOEY. That's true. Well, if we dance we've got to keep it simple.

---

*Please see Music Use Note on page 3.

ANGELINA. Simple.

(She does a sexy dance move.)

JOEY. None of that.

ANGELINA. Right.

(She does another sexy dance move.)

JOEY. Or that.

ANGELINA. We'll dance like all the old ladies and children.

JOEY. We'll have to.

(beat)

Some of them moves we did at Roseland...New Year's Eve.

ANGELINA. I remember.

JOEY. We got looks from the crowd.

ANGELINA. Were there other people at Roseland that night?

JOEY. A couple thousand.

ANGELINA. Didn't see them.

(beat)

Lovely night, Joey.

JOEY. It was perfect.

(During the following the song will fade away and the two will stop dancing.)

ANGELINA. When I got back home that night after Roseland, Joey, channel five was running these old movies. These black and white British films about, I don't know, British people. There were these five British guys and they're standing by this fireplace with glasses of champagne and one of them says, "To the Queen!" Then they drank their champagne and threw the glasses into the fireplace. And one guy, this American guy, he goes, "Why'd you do that?" And the British guy goes "So the glass can never be used again for a lesser purpose."

JOEY. Whoa!

ANGELINA. Like that?

JOEY. The British are so weird.

ANGELINA. Then I thought of my shoes, my dancing shoes, the ones I used that night. I jumped out of bed, marched out to the trash cans and I put them in there and that was that. My favorite dancing shoes, Joey. They cost forty-five dollars. They will never again be used for a lesser purpose.

JOEY. You remember how hot it got at Roseland? All them people? You got so hot you took off your stockings, shoved them in my pocket.

ANGELINA. I forgot all about that!

JOEY. I didn't. I found your stockings the next day. Now I keep them under my mattress. At night, when I go to bed, I reach down and I breathe them into my face. I smell them and you, your hair, your skin, you're all over me. It's you like you're right there in bed with me but you're not. I'm just holding stockings. Then I weep like a baby.

ANGELINA. You keep my stockings under your mattress?

JOEY. My mother found them. Now she thinks I like dressing up like a woman.

ANGELINA. Didn't you tell her where they come from?

JOEY. How can I? What can I say to her? "Ma, I've fallen in love with a woman who can never be mine so…"

ANGELINA. I'll always be yours.

(They kiss. As they kiss **PHIL** *enters from the back. He sees them kissing, turns right around and exits.)*

I worry all the time that John might kill me. Then I think he might kill you and I worry even more. I can't do this, Joey. There's no future for people like us. Not inside this family. And there's no way out. Not when there's guys like John around. We could get away with it for six months or a year but sooner or later, all we'd have to do is trip up once, just once, and it would be all over for us.

*(Suddenly we hear three gunshots right outside.
ANGELINA and JOEY duck as we hear LENNY scream.)*

LENNY. *(offstage)* Aaahhhh!!!

JOEY. What the…!

ANGELINA. Don't talk to me, Joey. It's over. I don't want to know you.

*(ANGELINA quickly exits to the ladies room as JOHN,
CARMINE and LENNY enter. LENNY is in a state of
shock as CARMINE holds up the Frisbee and examines
the two bullet holes he put in it.)*

LENNY. You people are insane!

JOHN. Aw, we were just havin' fun.

CARMINE. Lookit that, John. Two hits out of three. Nice shootin'?

JOHN. Very nice.

LENNY. That was my only sample! You didn't have to shoot it!

JOHN. Listen, fat guy…can I give you my personal opinion about this Frisbee thing? It's crap. It's a plastic piece of plastic crap that's never gonna catch on in a million fuckin' years.

LENNY. We weren't throwing it right. When you throw it you're supposed to *flick* your wrist. Kinda *flick* sorta.

CARMINE. Look at us. I'm serious. Look at us.

(LENNY does.)

Do any of us look like we're guys who "flick?"

JOHN. Leave your samples here. I'll call you tomorrow, tell you how much we want. And when you tell me how much it's costing me, I want to be *shocked* at how low your prices are. I mean fuckin' *shocked!*

CARMINE. John likes being shocked.

JOEY. Makes his day.

JOHN. I want to drop the phone! I wanna be absolutely, totally *shocked!*

LENNY. Shocked.

JOHN. That's right. Shocked in a good way.

LENNY. Uh huh.

JOHN. 'Cause if your prices are too high I might be shocked in a *bad* way.

CARMINE. You don't want that.

JOEY. Makes John cranky.

JOHN. And when I get cranky…

CARMINE. You don't want to know.

LENNY. Shocked.

JOEY. In a good way.

JOHN. We'll talk tomorrow.

(**LENNY** *forces a smile then exits.*)

(*Meanwhile* **ANGELINA** *enters from the ladies room. She stops at* **JOEY**'*s coat which is hanging on a coat hook. She furtively stuffs something in the pocket.*)

Angelina!

(*They both lose control and scream at each other.*)

ANGELINA. What! I'm right here! Jesus Christ, you don't have to yell at me like that! Like I'm some kinda piece of meat or somethin'! You're like an animal, John! An animal! Yell this! Yell that! No decorum or nothin'!

JOHN. How the fuck was I supposed to know you's there! Don't start! Don't start with me! Not now! You and your fuckin' attitude! I'm an animal?! Stop! Stop! Aw, you're breakin' my heart! Stop!

We gotta go, is all.

ANGELINA. We just got here.

JOHN. Well, now we're leaving.

ANGELINA. Where we goin'?

JOHN. Sheepshead Bay, c'mon.

ANGELINA. Where, that place again?

JOHN. Never mind what place. We're just goin'.

ANGELINA. You gonna make me sit outside again?

JOHN. Whatever! C'mon!

ANGELINA. Great, I get to sit in the car with the motor runnin' for two hours again. There's a fun night. You know what, John? You think you're audacious but you're not. You're fatuous is what you are. Every last bit of you is fatuous.

(*JOHN flashes with anger and grabs* **ANGELINA** *by her wrist.* **ANGELINA** *writhes with pain as* **JOHN** *seeks to put her in her place.*)

JOHN. What do you think? You think you're better than me all of a sudden?

ANGELINA. My arm!

JOHN. You think this two dollar book makes you better than me now?

ANGELINA. You're hurting me!

JOHN. You learn ten new words and now you're what? Smart or somethin'? Is that it? We can all kiss your ass now 'cause you learned ten new words?

ANGELINA. My arm! It hurts!

JOHN. I'll break it if I want! You hear me? You hear me!

ANGELINA. I hear you!

JOHN. You listen to me. You were trash when I found you, now you're trash in a mink coat! Don't you *ever* talk to me like that again! You understand? Not *ever*! You understand!

ANGELINA. Yes!

JOHN. I don't want to remind you of who you are again.

(*JOHN lets go of* **ANGELINA**. *She cries from humiliation as she runs out of the diner.* **JOHN** *watches her go, then exits after her.*)

(**CARMINE** *sees the look on* **JOEY**'s *face.*)

CARMINE. Joey.

(*No reply.*)

Joey.

JOEY. What?

CARMINE. Wipe that look off your face before someone sees it.

JOEY. What look?

CARMINE. The one that says you wanna kill John.

(**JOEY** *snaps out of it.*)

You in love with that girl?

(*beat*)

Are you in love with her?

(*No reply. Instead* **JOEY** *crosses to his coat and puts it on.*)

Jesus, Mary, and Joseph! You're in love with her! When you took her out last week did you bang her? Uh oh! I think you did. Either you banged her or she banged you or the two of you, you banged each other.

JOEY. Sometimes people fall in love, Carmine, without "bangin'."

CARMINE. (*news to him*) Like who?

(**JOEY** *reaches in his pocket and feels something he didn't expect to find. He takes out* **ANGELINA**'s *panties.*)

Oh, my God it's her underwear! She left you her underwear! Oh, that's sick! So sick! If John finds out he'll kill us both! Her underwear! Why the hell would you want her underwear! That's so twisted! That's…

JOEY. Shut the fuck up!

(**JOEY** *puts the panties away.*)

CARMINE. You gotta forget about her, Joey! You gotta put her out of your mind! We're plugged into this World's Fair thing now! Big time! We're in! We got it! No more nickels! No more trips to Hillbilly Land! We're gonna be rich! We're gonna make a fortune! We're on our way, Joey! We're gonna live like kings!

JOEY. Kings? You think we're gonna be kings? What king would watch a man strong arm the woman he loves?

That's what I did. I stood here and I watched that. She was in pain. She was in tears. I wanted to rip John's throat out with my bare hands but instead I stood here and I did nothing. I did *nothing*! Now you wanna call us kings? How could you possibly say that? Saying you're a king don't make you one. You can spend dough like a king, dress like one, eat like one, talk big like a king, drive a big car like a king but none of that don't make you one. You gotta *be* a king! Have the *heart* of a king! Have the courage of a king! The the the the guts and the bravery of a king! Stand face to face with what you know is wrong and risk your life to end it. You ever done that? I haven't. We ain't kings. We ain't nothin'. Haven't you noticed? Can't you tell?

(**JOEY** *exits as* **CARMINE** *looks on and the lights…*)

(Fade to black.)

Scene Two

*(It is several months later and the World's Fair has launched. **PHIL** has hung a banner that reads "Welcome World's Fair Visitors." World's Fair souvenirs are for sale at the counter, boxes containing World's Fair souvenirs are piled high where ever space permits and, if we can see it, a sign outside offers World's Fair parking for ten dollars.)*

*(As we begin **JOEY**, dressed in a tuxedo, sits at a table counting huge stacks of money. He's almost finished and keeps a tally on a slip of paper as he places the stacks of cash into a Macy's shopping bag.)*

*(**PHIL** is cleaning cutlery and a large assortment of knives, forks, serving spoons and carving knives are scattered about the counter.)*

(A lively song like "Poetry In Motion" plays on the jukebox.)

PHIL. You gonna dance?

JOEY. Hmm?

PHIL. I asked if you're gonna dance. You love this song. You used to dance to it every time it played.

JOEY. Don't have time.

PHIL. That's what happens when you start making money, kid. You stop doing the things you did for fun.

JOEY. Can't be helped. You got your parkin' lot money?

PHIL. All set to go.

JOEY. How's that comin'?

PHIL. Never thought I'd live to see it. People paying ten dollars to park their car in Queens. In the *bad* part of Queens. You know. The part where colored folks live.

JOEY. Aw, hey...c'mon...

PHIL. I'm kiddin'.

JOEY. How are the souvenirs doin'?

PHIL. Can't keep enough of them in stock. I run out of everything all the time. Word is you and Carmine are making it hand over fist.

JOEY. We're doin' okay.

PHIL. Just okay? Carmine bought himself a Cadillac, the official dream vehicle of Negros.

JOEY. It's a beauty, isn't it?

PHIL. How about you? When you buying a new car?

JOEY. I dunno. I drive by the Caddy showroom on Queens Boulevard, I slow down, I look…

PHIL. Listen to me. You're doing it wrong. You drive by, you slow down, you *stop*, you get out of that piece of crap you drive, go inside and buy yourself a Cad-illi-ack!

(mimes driving)

Mmm, mmm, *mmm*!

JOEY. *(laughs)* Okay.

PHIL. Tell the man "I want the leather and the eight track! Toss in a couple of blondes while you're at it! I want *all* the options!"

JOEY. When I go to buy, you come with me.

PHIL. I will. You could have gone to the wedding tonight in your new Caddy. Could have pulled up to the church in *style*.

JOEY. That's right. Jimmy Two Tone gets married in less than an hour. You goin'?

PHIL. Am I what? Am I what! Is a colored man going to an Italian wedding? Are you kidding? You can't be serious.

JOEY. Well, I…

PHIL. *(sarcastic)* Maybe I could dance with the bride while I'm there. Hold her close. Maybe run my hands up and down her ass. Give her a soul kiss. That'd be nice. People would love that! Then people can do that riddle I like so much: "What's black and white with six bullet holes in it." No, I'm not going to be the only colored man at a Sicilian wedding.

JOEY. Sorry. I wasn't thinkin'.

PHIL. It's all right. You're just young. You live in the world that's going to be. Not the one that is. Am I goin' to Jimmy's wedding. You're somethin' else.

(LENNY GREEN *enters from outside carrying a fairly large, cardboard box labeled "World's Fair T-shirts." He struggles over to a table where puts down the box and takes a breather.*)

LENNY. Damn, this thing gets heavier every time!

JOEY. You're makin' deliveries?

LENNY. It's the only way I can see any money out of this! I found out the trucking service gets twenty-two dollars to run a load out here. I told myself, "Hell, I've got a truck!"

PHIL. That T-shirts?

LENNY. Yeah.

PHIL. What else you bring?

LENNY. Beer steins and pennants.

PHIL. Snow globes?

LENNY. Tomorrow.

PHIL. You said they was comin' today.

LENNY. *(losing it)* Okay, so I fucked up! All right? So shoot me!

(panics instantly)

No, don't! It's just an expression! No shooting! I was just...I was...I tell you what. I'll bring the snow globes first thing tomorrow morning. Swear to God.

PHIL. Good enough.

(CARMINE *enters from outside wearing a God awful tuxedo.*)

JOEY. Whoa!

PHIL. Look out now!

LENNY. Wow!

JOEY. Mama!

(**CARMINE** *strikes some poses.*)

CARMINE. Huh? Huh?

PHIL. Lookin' good, Carmine!

CARMINE. You like?

LENNY. Very classy.

CARMINE. Huh?! Huh?!

PHIL. Some threads!

LENNY. Perfect fit.

CARMINE. Man, drivin' here in my new Caddy, wearin' this…I'm thinkin' to myself "I wish I had a camera! Someone, please take my picture!"

(**CARMINE** *strikes another pose.*)

PHIL. You look like one of The Four Tops.

CARMINE. Great. Am I gonna get laid tonight or what?

JOEY. You look so good I might fuck you myself!

CARMINE. Be gentle! I'm a virgin!

(**JOEY** *and* **CARMINE** *laugh and exchange playful punches.*)

PHIL. *(to* **LENNY***)* C'mon, I'll show you where that goes. You look great, Carmine.

CARMINE. Thanks, Phil.

(**PHIL** *exits into the back as* **LENNY** *follows carrying the box.* **JOEY** *finishes putting stacks of cash into the shopping bag.*)

How's the money lookin'?

JOEY. It's like a dam burst and I can't stop it from pourin' in.

(**JOEY** *shows* **CARMINE** *the slip of paper with the money count on it.*)

CARMINE. Holy shit! This for the week?

JOEY. That's for the last two days.

CARMINE. Mama! I keep tellin' you, Joey. We could skim ten percent, John would never miss it.

JOEY. And I keep tellin' you I like to *look* at the East River, not live at the bottom of it.

CARMINE. Still, it would be nice to have the extra dough.

JOEY. We're making ten times what we used to make, Carmine!

CARMINE. Still, I got my eye on a white Caddy.

JOEY. You just bought a Caddy.

CARMINE. The one I want is a convertible. I'm gonna use it to drive to and from my boat.

JOEY. You don't have a boat.

CARMINE. *(twinkles)* Not yet.

> *(then)*

> Listen, a couple dozen boxes of souvenirs "fell off the truck."

JOEY. Again?!

CARMINE. Yeah, and I ran outta room where I stash my stuff so I put this load in your garage.

JOEY. Aw, Carmine!

CARMINE. I didn't bother your mother. I know she's sick. I lifted up the door, put the stuff in, I took off.

JOEY. Carmine!

CARMINE. It's just for a while. It'll be there a day, maybe two. My guy from Jersey comes in, it'll be gone.

JOEY. Do me a favor, make this the last time. I mean it. If you wanna pick John's pocket, risk your life, fine. But don't involve me.

CARMINE. It's the last time. I promise. Now, c'mon. Lighten up. You look good. You might actually get laid at this wedding.

JOEY. Aw…

CARMINE. Hey, if a guy can't get laid at an Italian wedding he oughta hang up his dick and quit. You know how women get at weddings. All sentimental and horny. You talk to some chick, she says, "The bride is so beautiful!" You say, "I'd get married, too if I could find the right girl." Next thing you know you're bangin' her brains out in the men's room!

JOEY. That is so romantic, Carmine.

CARMINE. You know who's gonna be there? The Russo sisters. All three of them. You gonna bang one of the Russo sisters?

JOEY. Nah…

CARMINE. You're not gonna make me bang all three, are ya?

JOEY. I think so.

CARMINE. That's a lot of heavy lifting. You got your eye on someone else?

JOEY. No.

CARMINE. Well, you must have some sort of plan worked out for the wedding.

JOEY. I'm gonna sit and watch Jimmy and Tammy get married, go to the reception, have dinner, dance a little, drink a little, go home.

CARMINE. What the fuck kinda plan is that!

JOEY. It's my plan. It's what I'm gonna do, Carmine.

CARMINE. What about havin' fun? What about women? What about a little bah-bing?

JOEY. I'm not gonna bah or bing.

CARMINE. Sure you are.

JOEY. No, I'm not. I'm in love with someone, Carmine. With my whole heart and soul.

CARMINE. So?

JOEY. So nailin' some woman I don't even care about would be an infamnia…a disgrace. I could never do that to the woman I love. Never. I don't ask you to understand it, just respect it. It's how I feel about Angelina. I sent her flowers today. Two dozen white roses with a note that says I wished it was her and me gettin' married on this day. I wiped my tears with the card.

(**CARMINE** *is both stunned and touched. Finally…*)

CARMINE. I never loved anyone like that.

(beat)

What's that feel like?

JOEY. Right now, not so good.

(**ANGELINA** *enters on the run. She wears a bridesmaid's dress. She talks a mile a minute as she passes* **JOEY** *on her way to the ladies room, furtively looking outside throughout.*)

ANGELINA. Joey, listen, I only have a few seconds. I ran ahead. I told John I have to pee. When he came by my place to pick me up I went to get my purse in the bedroom for a few seconds. Then I remembered I never took your card off the flowers! When I come out John was standing right by the flowers but I don't know if he read the card or not! Christ! I am so sorry, Joey!

(**ANGELINA** *exits to the ladies room.* **CARMINE** *peers outside.*)

CARMINE. John's comin'. What are you going to do?

JOEY. Nothin'. Maybe he didn't read the card.

CARMINE. What if he did?

JOEY. *If* he did, I don't think I'm goin' to Jimmy's wedding.

CARMINE. Man! Everything was goin' so good, now this!

JOEY. Shhh! It's John. It's John.

(**JOHN** *enters dressed for the wedding.*)

CARMINE. Hey, look it's John!

JOEY. Hey, John.

CARMINE. Wadda yuh know, it's John! Heh heh! John of all people!

JOHN. What, you surprised to see me? Angelina just run in. I gotta drop her off before I pick up my wife! What! You think I'd pick up my wife with Angelina in the car? What kinda guy do you think I am! Huh?

CARMINE. No, I didn't mean it that way. I just mean it's great to see you, John. You look nice, John.

JOEY. Very nice.

CARMINE. Elegant. Real elegant, John. Il meglio. You're gonna be the best lookin' guy at this wedding.

JOHN. You think?

CARMINE. Fuckin' A.

(PHIL *enters from the back.*)

PHIL. Hey, John. You hungry? Something to eat?

JOHN. Naw… I'm on my way to a wedding. They got food there.

PHIL. Gotcha.

(PHIL *crosses to* JOHN *and hands him a letter sized envelope stuffed with cash.*)

Parking money.

JOHN. Fatter than last week.

PHIL. Looks like it.

JOHN. You take your cut?

PHIL. No, that's up to you. If you want to do that…That's not for me to do.

JOHN. *(to* CARMINE *and* JOEY*)* The man knows how to show respect.

(to PHIL*)*

I'll count this, get back to you later.

PHIL. Whatever you say, John. It's fine with me. Sure you don't want anything?

JOHN. I'm sure. They got food at the wedding.

(PHIL *nods and exits to the back.*)

JOEY. Money's all counted, John. Put away.

JOHN. How'd we do?

JOEY. Fantastic and it's only for two days. Weekdays, not even a weekend.

(JOEY *shows the tally slip to* JOHN.*)*

JOHN. Holy shit.

CARMINE. Huh? Huh?

JOHN. This is two days?

JOEY. Yesterday and the day before.

JOHN. Un-fuckin'-believable. Never in my wildest dreams did I think we could make this much money sellin' T-shirts an' snow globes.

JOEY. All of it in cash.

CARMINE. And it's totally legal except for the bribes, extortion, arson, and blackmail.

JOHN. Un-fuckin'-believable what we're pullin' in.

(**JOHN** *throws his car keys to* **JOEY.**)

Joey, be a good boy. Put the cash in my trunk.

JOEY. You got it.

JOHN. Put it under the mat. You'll have to take out the spare.

JOEY. Done.

JOHN. My car is down at the end of the lot. I didn't want no one puttin' a ding in the door. Fuckin' people in Queens don't give a shit about dings.

JOEY. I see it.

JOHN. You don't mind, Joey?

JOEY. Naw. Not at all, John. Right back.

(**JOEY** *exits outside.* **JOHN** *crosses to* **CARMINE** *and they sit at a table.*)

He don't mind at all.

CARMINE. Hmm?

JOHN. Joey…he says he don't mind.

CARMINE. What, runnin' out to your car? Neither would I. If you asked me I woulda. Be glad to.

JOHN. My wife tells me Rosey's got the flu.

CARMINE. Joey's ma… Yeah, he told me.

JOHN. I dropped by to see how she was. Drop off some cannoli. Pay a visit.

CARMINE. That's so like you, John. Caring about people.

JOHN. I parked in her driveway. On the way out Joey's mother says "Why don't you take the shortcut through the garage."

CARMINE. Uh huh.

JOHN. So I went out through the garage.

CARMINE. Yeah.

JOHN. Guess what I seen in Joey's garage.

CARMINE. I dunno.

JOHN. Go on, take a guess.

CARMINE. No idea.

JOHN. Take a guess!

CARMINE. Old tires?

JOHN. A hundred boxes of World's Fair shit. Stacked from the floor to ceiling. A hundred boxes.

CARMINE. Really?

JOHN. Maybe more. And all of it was stuff that's moving fast. Ash trays, pencils, pens, snow globes…Stuff we run out of all the time. Looks like Joey don't run out.

CARMINE. You sure?

JOHN. I know what I seen.

CARMINE. Maybe…

JOHN. Maybe what?

CARMINE. Maybe Joey's keepin' it there until it's time to sell it. You know, storin' it.

JOHN. We've got two storage spaces right near the fair. Neither one is full. My guess is this is swag Joey has stolen from me to sell on his own. I will only ask you one time, Carmine. Do you know anything about this?

CARMINE. Me? About the boxes? I uh…His garage, huh? You want to know if I…

(**ANGELINA** *enters from the ladies room.* **JOHN** *and* **CARMINE** *totally ignore her and she senses the tension.*)

ANGELINA. Oh, hi. I'll uh…I'll be over here.

(**ANGELINA** *crosses to another table where she sits.* **JOHN** *and* **CARMINE** *continue their uneasy silence. Finally…*)

JOHN. I said I would only ask you once.

(beat)

I'm waiting. Did you know?

(finally…)

CARMINE. No.

JOHN. Joey wanted this life. I never went to him. I never went to Joey and asked him to become part of this family. He came to me. He came to me and asked if he could be part of this. And I said I would give him this life. I would take him into my family and he would have all that comes with it. What did I ask of him in return? His brain, his hands, his mind, his soul? Did I even so much as ask him for his affection? Did I ask him for that? Not even. Not even. I asked Joey and guys just like him for one thing. Their respect. With that, everything else falls into place. I don't care if Joey sold a stick of gum behind my back. He has lost his respect for me. That means he has lost his place with us. He does not belong in my family. Not anymore.

CARMINE. John...

JOHN. He does not belong.

CARMINE. John, maybe if you...

JOHN. I seen Vincent.

CARMINE. Vincent?

JOHN. We talked. Vincent knows everything. Now I'm going to tell you something about Joey and this comes direct from Vincent. The capo di tutti capi.

(then)

Take my hand.

(No response.)

Take my hand.

*(**CARMINE** takes **JOHN**'s hand. **JOHN**'s grip is powerful and **CARMINE** winces with pain.)*

Joey does not live to see tomorrow.

CARMINE. John...

JOHN. Say it.

CARMINE. John...

JOHN. Say it.

CARMINE. He's my best friend.

JOHN. Say it.

CARMINE. …like my brother…

JOHN. Say it!

CARMINE. …not tomorrow…

(**JOHN** *lets go of* **CARMINE***'s hand.*)

John…

JOHN. Hmm?

CARMINE. Ever hear of the Yakuza?

JOHN. Who?

CARMINE. They're Japanese. They got this ceremony where they…

JOHN. *(interrupts)* Stop your bullshit! Do you wanna do this or do I go to someone else?

(**CARMINE,** *petrified with guilt and fear thinks for several long beats, finally…*)

CARMINE. I made a promise to Joey once. We made a promise to each other. If one of us ever had to go…it would come from the other.

JOHN. Then you get to keep your promise and you keep it tonight.

CARMINE. My tux, John…

JOHN. What about it!

CARMINE. I didn't bring a piece. It would ruin the shape of the tux.

(**JOHN** *takes out a gun and places it on the table.*)

JOHN. When you're done, you take over for Joey and keep his end.

(beat)

You should smile. Tomorrow you start makin' even more.

(**CARMINE** *stares at the gun then slowly picks it up. A beat then* **JOEY** *enters from outside.*)

JOEY. Done. I had to move the wedding present to one side, John.

(no reply.)

Big present. What is it? A punch bowl maybe?

(no reply.)

Well, the cash is under the mat next to the jack. Like you wouldn't see a bag that size!

(JOEY *crosses to the table to return* **JOHN***'s keys. He sees the gun.)*

What's up?

JOHN. I know what's goin' on, Joey. I know all about it.

JOEY. Know about what?

JOHN. What do you think?

(JOEY *looks to* **ANGELINA***. The two exchange looks of panic.)*

JOEY. When did you find out?

JOHN. Today. I found out today.

JOEY. Figures.

JOHN. They haven't invented the words that can tell you the shock and hurt I feel from all this.

JOEY. Well, I felt bad too, John. And I'm glad it's finally over. Hiding it was the most painful part. I've always loved and respected you. I never liked goin' behind your back. I just want you to know one thing, John. Angelina had nothin' to do with this.

JOHN. I never thought she did.

JOEY. Well, good 'cause she didn't. It was me. All me. I told her if she didn't go along with me, I would tell you that she *did* anyway. And she fought me, John. Oh, she fought me. Over an' over, she said no, it's not right, it wouldn't be right to do that to you. It wouldn't be fair. You've been so kind and generous to us both why betray you like that? But I kept at her with all kinds of threats until she finally caved in. It was me. It was all me. She's innocent. Totally innocent.

ANGELINA. No, I'm not innocent. Not innocent at all. I'm in love with Joey. Have been for a long time. Since I first seen him practically. Force me to go out with him? Force me to be with him? The only force he ever used was his smile. I love you, Joey.

JOEY. I love you, too.

(They smile at each other.)

JOHN. You two are having a thing?

JOEY. Yeah.

ANGELINA. That's what this is about.

JOHN. No.

JOEY. No?

JOHN. I found crates of World's Fair shit in your garage.

JOEY. Oh. So you…

JOHN. Not until now. Guess it's my lucky day.

(beat)

Carmine…

CARMINE. Here?

JOHN. Where ever you want. I just want it done. Both of them.

*(**CARMINE** gestures at the men's room.)*

CARMINE. C'mon… If I don't do it now…

JOEY. I know. You'll lose your nerve. At least we're keepin' our promise.

CARMINE. Yeah.

JOEY. I have to go, and it's going to come from you.

*(**CARMINE** nods then gestures with the gun. **JOEY** and **ANGELINA** look at each other, hold hands, then exit into the men's room as **CARMINE** follows. The instant **CARMINE** exits into the men's room we hear six gun shots. The shots are loud, almost deafening as we see flashes of light. **PHIL** and **LENNY** enter from the back having heard the gun shots. After several long, silent beats, **CARMINE** enters from the men's room, smoking gun in hand.)*

JOHN. Dead?

(**CARMINE** *nods.*)

The girl?

CARMINE. Hmm?

JOHN. Her, too?

(**CARMINE** *nods.*)

You sure they're dead?

CARMINE. Go in an' look if you want. But be careful. The floor's slippery. Blood. It's everywhere.

(**JOHN** *begins to feel sick to his stomach.* **PHIL** *prepares a stomach powder for* **JOHN**.*)

JOHN. Right.

CARMINE. *(pointing)* And don't trip on that thing over there…

JOHN. What thing?

CARMINE. It's a piece of Joey's skull. The bullet went up through his chin but come out the back of his head.

(**JOHN** *feels more sick.*)

Go on, take a look. A gun this size does a lotta damage. There's a hole in her…you can see daylight through it!

JOHN. Phil…go look for me…

PHIL. Excuse me, John?

JOHN. Go look. Tell me what you see.

(*As* **PHIL** *crosses to the men's room.*)

PHIL. First no snow globes, now this!

(**PHIL** *exits into the men's room for a few beats, then comes back out. All eyes are on* **PHIL**. **PHIL** *looks at* **CARMINE**, **JOHN** *and* **LENNY** *for several long beats. Finally…*)

Dead.

(beat)

Man, it'll take forever to clean up that mess.

(JOHN *feels more sick.*)

JOHN. Hnn!

PHIL. And her, well…She used to have a pretty face.

JOHN. Enough! I don't wanna hear no more!

PHIL. Sorry, John.

CARMINE. It had to be done, John.

JOHN. I know. Had to be. There's no way I could let an insult like that go unpunished.

CARMINE. I'll wait until late tonight, take them out to this place I know in Jersey.

JOHN. Fine.

CARMINE. I'll never get my trunk clean. No matter how much newspaper you put down it always soaks through. Brand new Caddy, too.

JOHN. I'll buy you another one.

CARMINE. No.

JOHN. I want to.

CARMINE. No, I couldn't.

JOHN. I insist.

CARMINE. Really?

JOHN. Whatever you want.

CARMINE. Did have my eye on a convertible.

JOHN. It's yours.

CARMINE. Well, thank you, John.

JOHN. *(re: LENNY)* What about him?

LENNY. *(petrified with fear)* What about me?

JOHN. You see any of this?

LENNY. Are you kidding? I wasn't even here! I was never here at all today. I haven't been out to Queens for days. In fact, I'm not even in New York City. I was with my wife and sister-in-law all weekend. We left early this morning for Atlantic City. We're still there. We're having a wonderful time, by the way.

CARMINE. *(to* JOHN*)* He'll be okay.

   (to LENNY*)*

   Walk John out to his car?

LENNY. Sure.

   *(*LENNY *escorts a weakened* JOHN *to the door.)*

CARMINE. You going to the wedding, John?

JOHN. Maybe later.

CARMINE. You rest up. Feel better.

JOHN. Thanks.

CARMINE. Tell Jimmy I'm sorry I missed his wedding.

JOHN. I'll make up an excuse.

CARMINE. Thank you.

   *(*JOHN *and* LENNY *exit.* CARMINE *calls after* JOHN*.)*

   I'll call you tomorrow after I bury the bodies.

JOHN. *(offstage)* Ooooh!!!

   (A beat, then JOEY *and* ANGELINA *enter.)*

ANGELINA. He gone?

CARMINE. John? Yeah.

ANGELINA. We heard what you did.

JOEY. Why'd you do that, Phil?

CARMINE. Yeah, how come?

PHIL. I've seen all the wiseguys in this family. For years. Each and every one of them stopped here on their way up or on their way out. Big guys, small guys, loud, quiet, half crazy, all crazy… Guys with gold teeth, gold jewelry, wads of cash so big one hand couldn't hold it all. Guys who carried guns, knives, shotguns, ice picks, baseball bats. Eyes like sharks. Cold blooded killers who could drink coffee, laugh and relax after just having choked someone to death. Brave men. All of them brave. But not so brave they would ever, not for one second, risk their life for a friend. I've never seen that. Not until now. Not until tonight.

   (beat)

PHIL. *(cont.)* You also ran cash and Christmas presents down to my sister and my nephews. Ain't a lot of white men who would do that. Take the time to stop and knock on my sister's door.

CARMINE. I never really knocked. I just slowed down, threw the presents out the window.

(PHIL smiles.)

PHIL. I'm going to take a nap. There gonna be any more "murders" tonight?

CARMINE. No, not tonight. I'm done with my killin' spree.

PHIL. Thank God.

(PHIL exits to the back.)

JOEY. Jeez, Carmine I thought for a second there you might...

CARMINE. I might what?

JOEY. You know.

CARMINE. No, I had enough of that.

(beat)

All I wanted to do was keep my promise to my best friend.

JOEY. If one of us ever has to leave...

CARMINE. It would come from the other.

JOEY. Now I've got to leave.

CARMINE. No one's gonna look for you, Joey. They think you're dead. But you'd better get dead and stay dead.

(They smile.)

Where you gonna go?

ANGELINA. Some place that has dancing.

JOEY. Yes, a place that has dancing.

CARMINE. *(to ANGELINA)* You wouldn't have a slutty sister by any chance, would you?

ANGELINA. Sorry.

(Without any warning **JOHN** *begins to enter the diner.* **CARMINE**, **JOEY** *and* **ANGELINA** *have less than a second before* **JOHN** *sees what's going on. In a flash* **ANGELINA** *drapes herself lifeless over a stool.* **JOEY** *drops into* **CARMINE** *'s arms lifeless as well.* **CARMINE** *picks up the largest carving knife he can find from the counter.* **JOHN** *enters.)*

JOHN. Carmine, before I forget…

CARMINE. John! You're just in time! We're gonna cut up the bodies!

*(***JOHN** *instantly feels sick.)*

JOHN. Never mind!

(He runs out of the diner holding his mouth.)

Aaarrrfff!

*(***CARMINE**, **JOEY** *and* **ANGELINA** *sigh with relief.)*

CARMINE. Close.

JOEY. Too close.

*(***CARMINE** *hands* **JOEY** *the keys to his car.)*

CARMINE. Here. Better not drive your piece of crap.

JOEY. You're kidding.

CARMINE. Take it. John's buying me a new Caddy anyway. C'mon, go. If someone sees you two, Phil and me get a family plot in Jersey. Go on. Beat it.

*(***JOEY** *hugs* **CARMINE** *goodbye.)*

JOEY. I knew you wouldn't.

CARMINE. Maybe my aim is just bad.

JOEY. Gonna miss you.

ANGELINA. I was wrong about you, Carmine. You're a prince. A kingly man.

CARMINE. You'd better scram. Take care of my best friend. Go scram. There's a full tank of gas.

*(***JOEY** *and* **ANGELINA** *begin to exit then pause at the door.)*

JOEY. Carmine, what's the stupidest name you ever heard?

CARMINE. Hands down, it's gotta be Bubba.

JOEY. If you ever get a postcard from Bubba... Maybe you'll wanna come visit?

CARMINE. I just might.

(*JOEY and* ANGELINA *laugh and exit as* CARMINE *watches them go.*)

Bubba...

(CARMINE *crosses to the jukebox, puts in a coin and a lively rock song plays. He dances. He dances badly – but he dances.*)

(*As he continues to dance, the lights...*)

(*Slow fade to black.*)

End Act Two

Also by
Jim Geoghan...

Light Sensitive

Only Kidding

OTHER TITLES AVAILABLE FROM SAMUEL FRENCH

LIGHT SENSITIVE

Jim Geoghan

Dramatic Comedy / 2m, 1f / Interior

Thomas Hanratty, lifelong resident of Hell's Kitchen and once the most dangerous white cab driver in New York, was blinded eight years ago in a drunken accident and is fading into a routine of self pity and alcohol. His bartender and only friend, who was partly responsible for the accident, is moving to Vermont with a new lady friend, but he can't abandon Tom. He recruits an unattractive, slightly-handicapped volunteer reader from the Lighthouse who battles her way through Tom's shell. By the second act, they are falling in love. His buddy returns with tales of his "Christmas from Hell" in Vermont, and doubt arises as to who will hold the number one position in Tom's life.

"Geoghan brings his characters to life and the audience to its feet cheering." – *Los Angeles Times*

OTHER TITLES AVAILABLE FROM SAMUEL FRENCH

ONLY KIDDING

Jim Geoghan

Comedy / 5m / 3 ints.

In this Off Broadway hit, an over the hill comic who is desperate for a shot on a late night TV show has invited a hip young writer to his cottage in the Catskills to help him update his act. They might as well be talking in tongues about what is funny! The second act moves to a seedy club where the mafia-connected owner wants aspiring comics to sign a contract giving him a commission on their future earnings. Then the play goes to comedy heaven: backstage at that late night TV show. The older comedian awaits his last chance at the big time and one of the comics from Act 2 is getting his first shot.

"[This] acidly funny dissection of the stand up comedy jungle...
crackles with authenticity."
–*The New York Times*

"A dazzling comedy. Fresh, clever and above all, funny."
– *New York Post*

"Might make you laugh so hard you won't appreciate what
fine writing it is."
– *New York Daily News*

"To be wise about being funny and still be funny is a rare
accomplishment indeed."
– *New York Newsday*